THE NIGHT BURNING

RITE WORLD: NIGHT WOLVES
BOOK 2

JULIANA HAYGERT

COPYRIGHT

This book is a work of fiction. Names, characters, places, and incidents either are products of the author's imagination or are used fictitiously. Any resemblance to actual persons, living or dead, events, or locales is entirely coincidental.

Manufactured in the United States of America.

First Edition August 2022

www.JulianaHaygert.com

Edited by H. Danielle Crabtree

Proofread by Jessica Nelson

Cover design by Claire Holt with Luminescence Covers

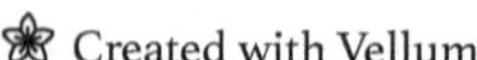 Created with Vellum

AUTHOR'S NOTE

RITE WORLD

Welcome to the RITE WORLD!

For a printable reading order, click here!

Free Novellas:
The Vampire Hunt
The Light Witch

Novellas:
The Hunter Path
The Light Calling
The Light Witch
The Wicked Alliance
The Shadow Fae

Rite World:
The Vampire Heir (Book 1)
The Witch Queen (Book 2)
The Immortal Vow (Book 3)
The Warlock Lord (Book 4)
The Wolf Consort (Book 5)
The Crystal Rose (Book 6)
The Wolf Forsaken (Book 7)
The Fae Bound (Book 8)
The Blood Pact (Book 9)

Rite World: Blackthorn Hunters Academy
The Demons Kiss (Book 1)
The Hunter Secret (Book 2)
The Soul Bond (Book 3)
The Shadow Trials (Book 4)
The Immortal Vow (Book 5)

Rite World: Vampire Wars
The Darkest Vampire (Book 1)
The Darkest Witch (Book 2)
The Darkest Magic (Book 3)

Rite World: Night Wolves
The Night Calling (Book 1)
The Night Burning (Book 2)
The Night Hunting (Book 3)
The Night Rising (Book 4)

Rite World: Lightgrove Witches
The Midnight Test (Book 1)

The Midnight Spell (Book 2)
The Midnight Flame (Book 3)

And more to come!

1

RAIKA

THE LAST QUARTER MOON SHONE BRIGHT IN THE CLOUDLESS night sky amid a heavy blanket of bright stars.

A beautiful night to say goodbye.

Wearing white slacks and a button-up shirt, Shane faced the large pyre erected in the center of the renovated main square. His new betas, Dom and Vallin, stood proudly by his side. Minsi and Tyren were a few yards to his right, Killian and Lavinia were to his left, and the rest of the pack surrounded them.

This time though, I was among them. Nestled between Rue and Roman and far from Serge and his friends, but I was here. With the rest of the pack for the first time in my life.

Shane picked up the torch from the floor. He extended it to the side, in Lavinia's direction. A second later, fire caught on the torch's top end.

I heard a few gasps go around the crowd. After the experience we had, most people here were wary of witches. Because of that, Shane always reminded everyone that Lavinia was now a vampire—with witch powers.

It had been seven days since the attack, five since the full moon was gone and Shane left the prison. I'd had lots of interaction with Lavinia since then. It was easy to talk to her and be around her because she looked and acted like a vampire most of the time. But then she did something like light a torch on fire with her magic and my gut clenched. I knew she wasn't like the Nightmist witches. Hell, she told me she had had a bad encounter with them last year, which was when she and Killian found Shane and helped him get away from them, but it was still hard to accept a witch was among us now.

The last time we allowed witches in our midst, things had gone terribly wrong.

I pushed past my prejudiced fears. Not all witches were the same, just like not all wolves were. I couldn't judge an entire species on the mistake of one group.

Shane held the torch high. "Tonight, we honor those who have fallen before. Their deaths won't be in vain." He lowered the torch. "Be with the moon."

He touched the torch to the pyre and the flames spread fast, becoming a huge white fire—the effect from a magical powder Lavinia added to the pyre.

"It eases spiritual pain," she had said.

We were all in need of that.

The pyre also had firewood the kids had collected yesterday with Rue and Vianna, and a bunch of other wolves and vampires—no one went anywhere without backup now. They went back to the library with the firewood and spent the day painting the names of the fallen and decorating them.

Shane lowered his head and we all followed his lead, giving our dead one full minute of silence and respect. I remembered my mother. She had been my best friend and died trying to protect me. I missed her dearly. I also forced myself to remember the others who had fallen in the first battle a year ago, and in the second a few days ago. Despite their hatred of me, I truly wished for them to find peace in death.

In silence, we watched as the pyre burned, embers flickering to the night sky.

I couldn't help but look at the handsome alpha standing behind the pyre. The flames gave his golden skin a deeper tone, and created shadows around the sharp angles of his face, making them look even sharper. The new alpha was too handsome for his own good.

Across the pyre and the crowd, his warm brown eyes met mine.

My breath caught.

In the five days he had been out of the prison, we'd barely had time alone. As alpha, everyone wanted to talk to him, ask him what to do next, and get his suggestions. To help him carry the weight of leadership, Dom and Vallin, one of the older wolves who had been good friends with his father, became his betas, and he had restored the council, which now consisted of only three wolves instead of ten. He wanted to appoint more wolves to the seats, but with only fitfy-ish wolves in the pack and one-fifth of those being kids, it wasn't like there were many choices. He appointed Killian as a temporary honorary council member because we needed the help.

Unfortunately, Serge was on the council and his first demand was to have me banished from the pack. His second was to send all the vampires away.

"We don't need trash in our midst, or vampires to help

out," he said. "We are Nightshade wolves. We are strong. We don't need anyone else."

I hadn't been there, since I wasn't on the council, but Killian told me Shane almost lost it. But Shane replied that I was staying, with an elevated rank, and the vampires were welcome and would stay. An argument started about Shane not listening to his council, and that he was too young and skewed by vampires and witches to lead us well, and that he was a forsaken Shadow Wolf who could turn against his people at any time.

Things weren't looking well in the Nightshade pack.

Besides all of that, Shane was a little disappointed with me. I had moved out of his house right when he moved in. He had argued with me, saying I could stay there with him and his siblings, that he wanted me there with them. He even used the Minsi-needs-you-here card.

The bastard. That had swayed me, but not enough. The three of them needed time alone, as a family, to reconnect and start over. Me being there would only make things awkward, messy.

We hadn't been truly alone since the day he told me about his curse when he was still in the cells underneath the town hall. I had been to his office a few times to deliver reports or get assignments, but people were always there. I had also dropped by their house when Minsi got anxious, but again, we had been with Minsi and sometimes with Tyren.

And that was another argument we had: our relationship.

Honestly, I didn't want to think about it, not yet, so I focused on my endless to-do list and went on with my day. And right now, I focused on the pyre between us and the objective of this ceremony: to send our loved ones away with honor and respect.

The fire receded to embers, and the wolves started moving around, greeting each other. Everyone here had lost at least one loved one during the battles.

To my surprise, a handful of wolves offered condolences for my loss—Jay, the healer; Vianna and her pups; Dom, Lucille, and Vallin; and two other elders whom I had intervene for before.

Well, that was progress.

Rue excused herself and went to help Vianna with the other kids. Minsi ran to me and Tyren came after her. I opened my arms for her. I would have hugged Tyren too, if he allowed me, but I settled for patting his shoulder once. Lucille, Dom, and Vallin were turning their backs to us when Shane approached our group.

Lucille maneuvered herself so she stood right beside Shane, her arm brushing against his. "That was a great ceremony."

"Thanks." Shane took a small step to the side, while looking at Minsi in my arms. I knew having Lucille clinging to him like that was annoying to him. It was equally annoying to me. "How is she?"

I shrugged. "Fine." She hugged me like this all the time, but Shane wasn't used to it. He thought she was always in distress. "That really was a great ceremony. You did well."

His eyes locked on mine. "Thank you. I wished we could do more, though."

"We can't rewrite the past," Roman said, sounding a lot wiser than he usually was. "We just need to take care of our future."

Shane's brows curled down. "We're working on that."

Maybe it was me, but I could feel the tension rolling off Shane as he regarded Roman. Since well before the first attack, when Roman started showing interest in me years ago, Shane had been watching. He had noticed, and he knew Roman's feelings for me hadn't changed.

He was jealous, and even though that was kind of cruel, I liked it.

I cleared my throat. "You know, it's late. Minsi should go to bed soon."

He nodded. Lucille reached for Minsi. "I'll help you take her home." Minsi hid herself behind me. "Or ... not."

"I'll do it." Tyren gently took Minsi's hands in his. Despite his teenage moodiness, he had been good with Minsi. He had even asked me to teach him some techniques to calm her down when she had one of her panic attacks, and I showed him what I knew.

Reluctantly, Minsi let Tyren hold her instead.

Shane looked at them. "I'll be right there." Tyren nodded and took Minsi away.

My heart tugged. I wanted to go with them, to help him put her in bed, read her a story, make sure she was all right. That Tyren was all right too. But I couldn't. I shouldn't. They had to learn how to live as a family, and if I interfered, they never would.

From the shadows, I saw two of Killian's vampires following Tyren and Minsi. I hated that she was still being followed anywhere she went, that we all were, but without the barrier to protect us, who knew what could happen? Anyone could come in at any time, and I couldn't stop thinking that Dixon had taken two crystals, but that wasn't the end of it.

I turned back to our group as Killian and Lavinia joined us, with Zin and Emil behind them—two of the vampires who usually patrolled the pack lands' border, where the barrier once was.

"Shane," Killian said, his tone grave. "We need to talk."

Shane's brow furrowed. "What is it?" Killian glanced at Lucille and Roman. "It's okay. I trust them."

"I was informed Whitecrest wolves were scouting outside Nightshade's borders."

Oh, no. "Didn't the Whitecrest meet with Conri?" Shane had told me that. He had learned about it when he met with Delco from the Ironfang pack.

"Yesss," Shane said, dragging the *S* out, thinking. "Are they still out there?"

"Three of them were still in wolf form when we came to warn you," Zin said.

He lowered his chin. "Let's go see if they are still there." He took a step forward, stopped, and glanced at me. As if remembering we weren't alone, he looked at Lucille and Roman too. "Excuse me." His gaze met mine once more before he went with the vampires. Dom and Vallin too.

Lucille crossed her arms and huffed. "Why can't women be betas? I could have been a nice one."

I smiled. "I'm sure you would, but Shane wanted to have one of the older wolves alongside him, so the rest of the pack will support him."

She glanced at me, her brows in knots.

"How do you know that?" Roman asked, the same question that was stamped on Lucille's face.

Shit. "I heard him talking to the others when they stopped by the library earlier to look at the records." Lies on top of more lies, but what I could I do? Shane and I had agreed not to tell anyone about us yet.

Lucille huffed and turned to look at where Shane and the

others were, crossing the main square, toward the other side of town.

"Well, I'm off too," she muttered. "Night."

"Good night," I said as she walked away.

Roman offered me his arm. "Shall we?"

I rolled my eyes at him and slapped his arm away in a joking manner, but I hoped he got the hint. It had been years and I still hadn't given in to him. Wouldn't he get it? I really didn't want to spell it out.

"We shall." I walked toward my house. Roman fell into step with me.

I glanced over my shoulder once more, but Shane and the others were already gone.

2

RAIKA

I knew I was having a nightmare but I couldn't wake up.

I was in a dark room with mirror walls, but I couldn't see my reflection because of all the shadows surrounding me. I reached for them, but each time I moved, they moved with me, as if retreating before I could touch them. A loud laugh echoed through the room and a flash of light came from the shadows, illuminating a silhouette: Conri.

A growl reverberated in the darkness. A flash of light. Another silhouette. Phell.

They took turns appearing among the shadows, laughing and growling at me, circling me.

The worst part was when more flashes of light sparked from the shadows. Minsi calling for me, her arms frantic as she reached toward me. My mother crying "no" as she fell on the floor. Rue pushing a metal cart like the one we had for so long. Roman being thrown against the wall.

And Shane in his Shadow Wolf.

He broke off from the shadows and advanced on me, his teeth bared, his claws poised to strike.

"Shane, no," I whispered. "It's me."

He rushed to me, his arm coming up for a strike.

I closed my eyes and braced myself.

A sound woke up and I sat in bed, breathing hard.

What the … ?

A loud, insistent knock came from the front door. Alarmed, I bolted from my bed and raced down the stairs. The knock came again but I opened the door a second late.

"What …" I stared at Shane. "What time is it? What are you doing here?" My eyes drifted down his body and I snapped them back. "You're naked!" That was when I realized I was wearing thin shorts-and-top pajama set. I crossed my arms, as if I could hide anything.

"Sorry, I had no time, I shifted and came." His voice and the hard set of his mouth said he was in distress.

"What is it?"

He ran a hand over his messy hair. "Minsi. She's having a panic attack. Tyren and I are trying to calm her down, but nothing is working. I didn't know what else to do."

"It's okay." I glanced back at my house, pondering what to do for a moment. "I'll go with you but, hm …"

"Just take off your clothes and shift," he said. Nakedness was a normal thing for wolf shifters, but I felt self-conscious being naked in front of him. "It's faster this way. You can get dressed again once we get there."

I bit down on my lower lip but nodded. I stepped onto the porch and closed the door behind me. Shane turned his back to me and I also turned my back to him before I was tempted to stare at his round, firm ass. I mean, it wasn't as if I hadn't before, but I didn't know … I still felt a little shy about all of this.

Pushing those ridiculous thoughts from my head, I slipped off my pajamas, put them on the couch on the porch, and shifted.

I inhaled deeply, letting the crisp night air fill my lungs and energize my blood. I'd had free access to my wolf for a week now, and even though I had shifted at least a dozen times since, it still felt like a dream. That I had to enjoy it while I could, because this dream could turn into a nightmare at any time.

Ready? Shane asked in my mind.

I turned and found he had already shifted, and his big black wolf twice the size of mine.

Yes, I told him.

Together, we ran back to his house. The front door was wide open and we went right in. In the foyer, we shifted back into our human forms. With our backs to each other, we picked up clothes from the coat closet—Shane put on runner's shorts, and I grabbed one of his mother's summer dresses. He had put several of his mother's old clothes there for me, just in case. I had teased him at the time, questioning his reasoning.

I should have known.

Shane and I climbed the stairs to the second floor and found Tyren with Minsi in her bedroom. Minsi sat on her bed crisscross applesauce, rocking back and forth and muttering nonsense words, while Tyren sat beside her and rubbed her back.

He saw us entering the room and jumped up. "Thank the moon you're here."

I walked around him. "Has she been like this since it started?"

Tyren and Shane shook their heads.

"She had a nightmare," Shane told. "She came to my room to tell me, but I think it started then. She began crying and couldn't even tell me anything. That was about forty minutes ago. I brought her to bed, stayed with her. She seemed to relax for a couple of minutes, but then she started screaming."

"It sounded like someone was ripping her limbs apart," Tyren said. "She stopped, started rocking like this, but she had another screaming fit."

Shit, it hadn't been this bad in a while. "I'll see what I can do." I glanced at Tyren. "Could you bring me some ice, please?"

Tyren frowned. "Sure." He walked out of the room.

"Ice?" Shane asked from the doorway. He hadn't entered the room.

"The shock in temperature helps to break the cycle," I explained. "Sometimes it works, sometimes it doesn't." I sat beside Minsi, facing her. "Hey, girl. I'm here."

Minsi's rocking slowed, and after what felt like an eternity, her gaze shifted to me. "Raika," she whispered. She threw herself on me and wrapped her thin arms around my neck tight.

"Hey, hey, I'm here." I adjusted her in my lap and embraced her shaking body. Minsi was such a small girl, it sometimes scared me. She didn't look eleven years old. With her short height and frail frame, she looked more like seven, if not six years old. "Everything is all right now." I smoothed my hand down her back as she continued to rock in my lap, and hummed in her ear.

Tyren came back with a glass full of ice. I picked up two ice cubes, mouthed "thank you," and disentangled Minsi's arms from their death grip around my neck. I placed the ice cubes in her hands. She gripped the ice and her breath hitched. I moved us around, laying her down in bed and snuggling beside her.

"I'm here, pretty girl. You're okay. Try to sleep." I placed a kiss on her forehead and she nestled her head in my shoulder.

I shooed the boys away. I wasn't sure of the time, but I knew it was the middle of the night, and both of them should be sleeping. Shane and Tyren disappeared from the bedroom.

A minute later, Minsi's body became heavy against mine, and I picked up the ice cubes from her hands before they melted and soaked her pajamas and her blanket, and placed them back in the glass.

Shane came back with his pillow. He sat down with the pillow between his back and the dresser, facing the bed. I lifted my eyebrows, as if asking what the hell are you doing, but he wasn't fazed. He kept staring at Minsi and me. Creep. I tuned him out and tried relaxing beside Minsi. Usually, the dozens of times I had snuggled in bed with her like this, I had ended up sleeping too.

But this time, I didn't. I continued humming to her, even though I knew she was finally sleeping, and thought about her. Poor girl. We needed to do something more for her.

Jay was our healer, but besides being the apprentice before the first attack, he didn't know anything about panic attacks. Witch potions only went so far. They were like cold medicine. They treated the symptoms in the moment, but they couldn't cure the root of the problem. Minsi needed real medical treatment, with a real human therapist.

The problem was how we would do that.

After about thirty minutes, when I was sure she was out for the rest of the night, I disentangled myself from her. Shane, who also hadn't slept, shot up and helped me get out of her bed without waking her up. On tiptoes, we left her room, went downstairs, and stopped in the kitchen.

"Want some water?" Shane opened the fridge. "Or maybe some beer?"

"How about some tea?"

Shane turned to the kettle over the range. "Tea it is."

While he fussed over my tea, I sat on one of the stools around the island. It was so strange to be back here. This had been my kitchen, my home for the past year, and now it wasn't. However, this place held bad memories.

When Shane first witnessed one of Minsi's panic attacks, I talked to him about this afterward. This house was complicated for her. It held her parents' memories, but it also held Conri's, Dixon's, and even Lorie and Keeva. Right now, the bad memories were winning over the good ones.

He had agreed and immediately started renovations—the walls were being painted, some furniture had been tossed out, and now they were waiting to buy some new pieces, and even the decorations and mundane kitchen things were being replaced. But it would take time for the changes to be complete. Meanwhile, Minsi still associated this house with the bad stuff.

Shane brought over two steaming mugs. He placed them on the island before sitting down on the stool beside mine. He turned my stool so I was facing him, and pulled his stool closer.

His eyes fixed on mine. He placed his hand on my knee, leaning over me. A small smile tugged at my lips and I met him halfway. His lips brushed against mine, a soft flutter, and then they were gone.

"That's better." Keeping his hand on my knee, he picked up his mug with his other hand, and took a sip of his steaming tea.

I frowned. That was it? We barely had any time alone lately and that was how he kissed me?

I grabbed my mug, taking a careful sip so as not to burn myself. Chamomile and vanilla, my favorite. "Thank you."

"Thank *you*." He put his mug down and scooted closer to me, his legs straddling mine. "I mean it. I don't know what to do when she has these attacks. If it weren't for you ..." He shook his head once. "See? You should be here. Living in this house with us."

I stared at my mug for a second. "Shane, we've talked about this."

"I'm changing my mind," he said, adamant.

I chuckled. "No, you're not changing your mind. You never really agreed with me. You just went along with it because you knew I wouldn't concede."

"You know me so well." He flashed a dazzling smile.

Dear moon ... we were alone in the darkness of the kitchen with the brightness of the moon outside illuminating everything, and he was wearing only shorts, exposing his glorious torso, shoulders, and arms. And I wasn't wearing any underwear underneath this dress.

Didn't he know how easy it was for him to disarm me when he smiled like that?

I cleared my throat. "You're saying that because of Minsi."

"That is a big reason, yes, but you know I want you here ... with me." He squeezed my knee.

"If I move back in, people will talk." Just like they talked when I lived here with Conri. Many still believed I had been his woman, no matter what I said or did. "They will see me here and they will assume we're together."

"Maybe that's not such a bad thing, seeing as you're my mate."

I put my mug beside his. "Shane, we are in such a precarious situation right now. Our numbers are low, and a handful of significant wolves are wary of you for many reasons, but mostly because of your Shadow Wolf. You don't want to add fuel to the flames by telling them you're mated to the pack's omega."

His lips pressed into a thin line and his jaw ticked, the way it always did when he was irritated. "I don't care about your rank. Besides, after all you did for the pack? They should be worshipping the ground you walk on."

I shook my head. "It isn't easy to change a lifetime of habits and perceptions."

"I already announced I'm changing your ranking in the next official council meeting."

"And that caused Serge and the others to voice their discontent. Imagine when you actually do it. Then you tell them you're mated to me? They might as well challenge you."

His eyes darkened, his hands clenched into fists. "I would like to see them try."

I reached over and placed a hand on his chest, right above his heart. "Don't you want to be a better alpha? A fair alpha who listens to everyone? Then you can't ignore what they are saying and threaten them."

Shane let out a long sigh and rested his hand over mine. "My mother told me you were wise and you would be a great mate for me. She was right, as usual." Shane's arms reached out, and in a flash, I had moved from my stool to his lap, my legs around his waist, my hands clutching his shoulders. I almost yelped with the sudden movement, but thankfully, I kept it in. "You're right, I know that. I'll change your ranking, give them time to get used to it, and then we'll fix the other problems—"

"Mainly, your curse."

"Mainly, my curse. And then, I'll tell everyone about us." His hands closed around my waist and held me tight against him while he shifted his waist, rubbing my hips to his. I gasped. "Because, damn it, I want you like this all the fucking time."

One of his hands clasped the nape of my neck as he pulled me to him. His mouth claimed mine and I swallowed a moan as I opened up to him and kissed him back. His lips were warm and soft, and his taste was of chamomile and vanilla, mixed with the mint of his toothpaste. His scent wrapped around me, that warm jasmine aroma I couldn't resist.

Good thing I had brains too, because I remembered we were in his house with his siblings, and I wouldn't be doing anything while we could get caught.

It was a herculean effort to break the kiss, push away from Shane, and take two steps back. "Don't," I whispered, not trusting my voice. By the moon, I wanted to have sex with him, but not like this. "Not when your brother can walk in on us."

"He wouldn't come downstairs," Shane said. A small, knowing smile curved his lips. "He would have heard us from his room and stayed in there, probably with some music to muffle everything."

"Oh, by the moon." I pressed my hands to my flaming cheeks.

Chuckling, Shane rose and walked to me. He grabbed my wrists, pulling my hands down and my arms around his waist. He leaned into me. "I'm teasing you."

"I know and I hate I can't stop myself from falling for it." I rose on tiptoes and pressed my lips to his. "I hate you."

"No, you don't." Shane pushed me against the kitchen counter and kissed me again, deeper this time, harder, more insistent. A warmth like no other traveled down my body and lodged low in my belly.

Moon, this was just too good.

Shane's hands slid down around my hips, to the dress's hem. His fingers grazed against the skin of my thighs and I gasped against his mouth.

The click of a door closing came from upstairs, and Shane and I stilled. We waited for a few seconds, but when no one presented themselves, I decided it was enough. That could have only been Tyren, trying not to hear us.

Though we hadn't told him the truth, Tyren knew about us. At least that was what I assumed with the way he treated me, or looked at us, as if he was in on a secret. Still, I didn't want to scar him for life by listening to his brother and me while we … yeah.

I pushed hard against Shane so he would release me and walked to the other side of the kitchen. "Stay there," I told him, my voice low.

He crossed his arms, his lips curled up. "Yes, ma'am."

I shook my head. "I'll see you tomorrow."

"Wait." He ran a hand through his hair. "Tomorrow evening, let's go for a run. Just you and me. I'll talk to Rue, she can stay with Minsi and Tyren. And I can talk to Killian and Lavinia too. They will cover for us."

My cheeks flamed with the prospect of spending the

evening with Shane running with our wolves. "Sure. I would like that."

"I'll text you the details later."

I nodded, and before I lost my cool and changed my mind, I turned and left the house.

3

SHANE

I always hated when Raika walked away from me, even if I agreed with her reasoning. After she left, I went back to bed —alone and with a massive hard-on—and tried to rest a little. In the end, this ordeal with Minsi had lasted almost two hours ... two precious hours of sleep I really needed.

Since getting out of the prison after the full moon, I worked with everyone nonstop. There was so damn much to do around here. Most nights, I had only four or five hours of sleep. That might be enough for some people, but it definitely wasn't for me. The lack of sleep was building up. I felt grumpy and irritated, and sometimes about ridiculous things.

Next morning, my day started with a lengthy surveillance of the pack lands' borders. I met Killian outside the house he and Lavinia were staying in, and together, we ran along the former boundary—me in wolf form and he with his vampire speed.

Last night, when Zin informed us the Whitecrest wolves had been around, I'd gone out ready for a fight. It didn't come to that, but I had seen the last three wolves surveying the area as they ran away, back to their pack. That made me uneasy.

What the hell did they want? What had they planned with Conri? What had Conri promised them? I hoped it wasn't something like "you can have a part of their lands if you deliver me the alpha's head" because my pack wasn't ready for a new battle. The barrier had spoiled us, made us dependent on it. Without it and with our numbers so low, anyone could attack us and we wouldn't be able to do shit.

To help better our odds, the next thing on my to-do list was to oversee a training session with our soldiers, and to take stock of who wanted to join our army.

Most of the male wolves were waiting for me in the biggest clearing in the pack lands—Dom, Vallin, Roman, Serge and his friends. Jay had tried joining the day before, but I had told him he was our only healer. He needed to save the injured wolves and leave the fighting to us. He seemed relieved.

And then there was Tyren.

Every day, he and Hugh, a boy of fourteen who had lost his parents in the first attack and now lived with Vianna and the other kids in town, came to training.

And every day, I turned them down.

Today, my grumpiness was high. I stomped into the clearing and got in his face. "Are you deaf?"

Tyren, who would soon be as tall as I was, puffed his chest and kept his gaze on my chest. "No, but I'm young and strong, and I can fight." His eyes lifted briefly, meeting mine. "Let me do this, Shane. I want to. If it were you, you would have wanted this too."

I opened my mouth to argue, but Killian nudged my

shoulder with his. "The boy has a point. You would have done the same."

It was true. I would have, and the sick thing was that if my father were here, he would have been proud of me for wanting to protect the pack. Well, to be totally fair, I had been allowed to train with the army at fifteen, though I only started joining missions and fighting after I was eighteen.

But that was because I had been the alpha heir. My father had wanted to prepare me to be a good leader.

Right now, Tyren was my heir.

Deep down, I did feel pride for Tyren's initiative and willingness. For his strength and courage, but after all we went through, the idea of putting him in danger shook me to the core. Because this wasn't training like when I was his age. No, this was real training. With the crystals gone, with my curse still hanging over our heads, it was only a matter of time before trouble found us.

And I didn't want him in the midst of it.

But butting heads wasn't working. We had been apart for a year. He was having a hard time wrapping his head around the fact that I didn't leave because I wanted to. That I was kidnapped and taken from them.

I let out a long sigh. "You two can stay and train. However!" I lifted one finger and stared at both of them. "That doesn't mean you will fight. If it comes to that, you *will* listen to me, and if I tell you to stay back, you will. Do you understand?"

"Yes, sir," Tyren and Hugh said in unison.

I shook my head but decided to let it go for now. After that, we trained. I stayed with the novices, while Dom and Vallin helped the veterans. Killian also helped, suggesting tactics and maneuvers we hadn't thought about. Vampire tricks that might came in handy.

After training, we separated for an hour. While the others rested before our next task, I went into my dad's office in the town hall—my office now—and had a quick lunch while reading reports and listing more things to do. Fix this town, protect my people, find the crystals, break the curse ... it felt like the list would never end.

It probably wouldn't. I hadn't paid much attention, but my father seemed to be busy, taking care of the pack. I hoped it got better, because I wanted to have some free time to spend with my family, with my mate.

I had sent a message to Rue, asking her to stay this evening with my siblings, and she had replied she would be glad to. I put my next plan into action: I carved out twenty minutes of my lunch-reading-reports time to set up things for tonight.

It wasn't much, but I hoped she liked it.

On my way back from the forest, Killian found me and walked back to town with me. Several times, I had told him and Lavinia that they didn't need to stay. This wasn't their fight, their problem. The two of them had finally found their happily ever after, but it hadn't lasted six months because of me. But they insisted they wanted to be here, they wanted to help—until we had the barrier back up, at least.

"Then we'll come for visits," Lavinia had teased. "And you better visit us too."

Once things settled down, once the barrier was back up, once the curse was gone, and my people were secure and happy, then, only then, would I visit friends.

"I received news from Taos," Killian said, bringing me back to the present.

As a prince of DuMoir Castle, Killian had many vampire warriors under his command, and right now he was using a bunch of them to help us. I would be forever grateful for that, because without them, we wouldn't have enough hands to get everything done.

Taos was one of Killian's vampires and he had been sent to track down Dixon and the crystals.

"And?"

"He hasn't seen Dixon, but he talked to some people who had. He thinks he's a day behind Dixon's trail."

"Good." I nodded. Finding the crystals, putting them back, and bringing the barrier back was top priority.

Not just because of our safety, but because of everything the barrier did for us: It kept the frigid, northern Canada weather out, and it created a better schedule for our day— the sun had always set at seven in the evening on the dot, even though outside it varied from four thirty in the winter, and ten at night in the summer. It was June now, which meant we were closer to sun setting at ten, and that was unsettling. At least the weather wasn't bad, though the air was already a lot chillier than before and the plants were showing signs of distress. We needed to find the crystals before winter came; otherwise it would be impossible to stay here.

We walked toward the main square, skirting the edge of the burned part of town. I didn't know what to do with it. At some point, after everything else was done, we would have to just take it all down, dispose of it, and build some new houses. Not that we needed them right now, with our numbers, but in the future ... hopefully, our numbers would increase.

Killian and I arrived at the main square five minutes late.

The wolves were already working, without me needing to tell them what was next on the agenda. That was a relief.

Some cleaned up the school so the kids could have classes there instead of in the library. Others painted the houses different colors and fixed broken porch steps or windows. It wasn't just inside my house that we wanted to forget the demons were ever here.

It was everywhere.

Without a word, I picked up a paintbrush and joined them.

Lucille worked on the flowerbed lining the streets, planting new flowers and shrubs. Tyren and Hugh helped her, and from the way they kept looking at her and grinning, I knew they couldn't care less about the flowers.

At least now she was busy with them and wasn't paying attention to me. Since she had been freed, Lucille had been incessant. She'd come to the prison to visit me more than Raika. When I moved back to my house, she came over often to check on me and my siblings, and brought homemade meals for the three of us. Sometimes during the day, she came to my office and brought me coffee. And every time, she touched my arms and stood closer than necessary.

I appreciated the help and the goodies, but I knew she wasn't doing that out of the goodness of her heart. She did it because she was interested in me, always had been, and she wanted my attention.

Many times during these past few days, I had thought about talking to her, telling her the truth, letting her down nicely, but I was afraid of her reaction. Right now, she treated Raika nicely, as if the two of them could be friends in the future—which was surprising. I never thought Lucille could be kind to Raika. But there it was and I was so afraid that if she found out the truth, she would turn against Raika and bully her again. Worse, Lucille had great influence over the females in the pack. She could turn all of them against Raika.

Like a coward, I didn't do anything about it. I let her come on to me as if she had a chance, though I didn't encourage her. I hoped that when she found out, it didn't hurt her too much.

I shook my head and turned my attention back to my task, but it didn't last a minute. Roman, who had been fixing a broken fence, ran past me, toward the main square.

No, not the main square. The library. Just as Raika stepped out carrying two heavy bags around her shoulders and more books in her arms. My gut clenched as I watched her, so pretty and radiant with her rebel style. Today she wore ripped jeans shorts, a cropped top with her short leather jacket, and combat boots. Her long, black hair was loose behind her back, the waves full and reaching down to her waist. Even from here I could see the shine of her bright blue eyes and the smile she offered Roman when he took one of the bags and books from her.

The bastard ...

"Hey." Killian put a hand in front of my chest. "Wake up."

I looked down at myself. My fists were clenched, the paintbrush held like a weapon, and I had taken two steps toward Raika and Roman.

Shit. "Thanks," I muttered, but I couldn't relax. I couldn't not look as Roman walked my mate across the main square, smiling and talking to her like an idiot.

I had always known he liked her. He had been trying to get in her pants for a while now. If only he knew she was my mate. Soon. Soon, when things calmed down, when we solved a few problems, then everyone would know what

Raika was to me, and Roman wouldn't dare smile at her anymore. Not like this.

They entered the school, and with a grunt, I turned back to the wall that wasn't going to paint itself.

"You trust her, don't you?" Killian asked, his voice low so the two of us could hear it. I dipped my chin once. "Then relax. Nothing will happen."

I did trust her. I didn't trust other males. Raika was pretty, sweet, and she didn't impose herself as she once did when others backed her to a corner, because she was afraid of disrupting the pack's peace.

I exhaled, reminding myself once more that that would change soon too.

4

RAIKA

SHANE THOUGHT I DIDN'T NOTICE HIS REACTION, BUT I DID. Even with several yards between us, I saw the way he tensed and turned the moment Roman reached me as I left the library with some of the school's supplies.

I had to admit that when I pushed aside all that stupid male dominance thing, I liked seeing him jealous and protective. I never had that before, and coming from him, if felt special.

I also had to admit that when it was the opposite, when Lucille was all over him, I hated it. So I behaved myself. I treated Roman as I always did—kind and friendly—but I made sure I didn't cross any lines so he wouldn't misunderstand things.

I glanced at Shane once while crossing the square with Roman, but at that moment, he was looking at Killian, talking to him.

Several thoughts flooded my mind.

About Killian and Lavinia and their vampires staying and

helping us, even though they didn't have any obligation to do so.

About how much work Shane had ahead of him, and how I would do anything I could to help him too.

About how it had been painful to leave him last night when all I wanted was to have fallen in his bed with him and spent the night there.

Keeping my distance from him and his siblings was proving to be hard. But it was necessary. Not just because the three of them needed time by themselves, but also because of the pack. Shane knew I was right. We had to keep up appearances for now.

Roman and I entered the school and went to the front office on the right. The sound of hammering, sawing, and footsteps came from upstairs, where a group of wolves worked on fixing the classrooms and building new desks.

"Where do I put these?" Roman asked.

"Here." I set the bag I was carrying on the large desk behind the counter.

He placed the bag and the books on the desk too. "What now?" he peeked inside the bags. It was notebooks, pencils, markers, and everything else we would need to start actual school again. Dom had retrieved them yesterday from the nearest town, where we had an address for mail and orders we placed.

"Well, there are two more bags in the library."

He chuckled. "I'll go get them."

Roman sauntered out of the school and I looked around at the office. While we were enslaved in our town, the demons had occupied several rooms in the school and made a mess of them. We had tossed the broken furniture and stained rugs, and now the rooms looked bare. This one had the built-in counter, a desk, and a file drawer, which had been bent somehow, but Shane had hammered it back into place. It wasn't perfect, but it would do until the new furniture arrived.

We had also ordered new computers, laptops, tablets and more—not just for the school, but for the entire pack—since the demons had broken or disposed of those. Those would be arriving tomorrow.

My phone dinged and I almost jumped out of my skin. I had been without a phone for over a year, and now that I had one back, it was hard getting used to it. Though most would receive new phones tomorrow with the laptops and whatnot, Shane had made sure a few of us had phones right away. Killian and Lavinia had gone out on the first day after the battle and bought phones for Tyren, Dom, Vallin, Lucille, Rue, Vianna, and me.

When Serge saw me with a phone in my hands when he didn't get one, he almost lost it. He had called me scum in front of half of the pack. Not wanting to cause more trouble, I remained quiet, ignored him, and kept cleaning up the main square. Since Shane was locked in the prison, he had asked Dom and Vallin to intervene, threatening to shut Serge up with the alpha command.

That had worked.

For about six hours.

I fished my phone from my jacket's pocket and glanced at the screen. Rue had texted me a picture of the kids around the library rug, doing crafts. And right in the back, lying on the pillows, Minsi, with her nose stuck in a book.

I couldn't blame her. She was at the library surrounded by pure treasure, and Rue wanted her to color? Nuts!

Grinning, I texted back laughing and a heart-eyes emoji.

I put my phone back into my pocket and started unpacking the school supplies. The idea was to separate them and put them in backpacks, all ready for the kids. When they came for the first day of school, they would receive their backpacks.

I wanted to do something special for them, but I didn't know what yet. Personalized notes that they found when they opened their bags? Little keychains for them to clasp on the bag's zipper? I was still thinking of ideas.

The sounds from upstairs stopped and I frowned. It was the middle of the afternoon. Perhaps whoever was upstairs would take a break. Or do something else. The moon knew there was enough work in town to last us an eternity.

I separated the school supplies in piles around the desk. One of the bags Roman was bringing next had the backpacks, then I would be able to just put everything inside and—

"Look, the omega," Serge said as he rounded the corner and stopped a few feet from the front office's counter.

My blood chilled.

The damn wolf had always been mean, but now he blamed me for the death of his buddy, Lonan. He was meaner than ever. I glanced at the two other wolves flanking him, Ian and Buck. They had always been around Lonan and Serge, and though they hadn't done anything to me, they had encouraged the others.

They were all sick bastards.

With slow steps, Serge approached the counter and I did my best not to step back. Serge was in his eighties, but because of wolf genes, he didn't look a day over forty. He wore a full black beard, probably to compensate for the lack of hair on the top of his head, and he had a bit of a beer gut. Though

I had no idea how he managed to keep that up when eating one meal a day for the last year.

He had probably drank barrel after barrel to compensate for not having any for a year.

"You should be scrubbing the floors, scum." He leaned over the counter, his eyes leaving a nasty trail over my body. I fought the urge to cover myself. "On your fours." He licked his lips.

I pointed to the front of the school. "The door is that way."

"You should go," he said. "Wasn't that what we said? That you and your family should leave the pack? Well, your family is dead, nothing we can do about them now." He glanced at the men behind him and the three of them chuckled. "But there's no barrier now, and we lost so many. Losing one more won't make a difference."

I buried my heels on the floor and held a notebook tightly in my hands.

Once upon a time, I had wanted to leave. When I started helping Shane, I had even thought about it, that once we freed the pack, I would leave ... but that was before everything had changed.

"Leave me alone, Serge," I said through gritted teeth. "You don't want to get in trouble with me."

Serge let out a dry chuckle. "Trouble with you?" His eyes settled on my legs for a second too long. "Maybe I do. Aren't you a whore? You probably know all the ways to get us into trouble. Maybe I'll do just that before making you leave."

Rage coursed through my veins and I flung the notebook at Serge's face.

It hit him squared on the nose. "Why—you *whore*." He rounded the counter, coming for me.

My rage escalated and I stood my ground. I would teach this old man some manners—

A cold sliver rushed down my back as the overhead lights flickered and went off. Shadows covered my hands. I lifted my arms and—

"What's going on?" Roman demanded as he stepped inside the school.

Clarity came back to me, filling my chest with shame, and I hid my hands behind my back.

By the moon, what had I almost done?

Roman dropped the bags on the floor, Lavinia appeared behind him, her eyes on me, and Serge stepped back, toward his friends.

Serge put a hand over his nose. "The omega threw a book at me!"

My mouth fell open. That was so childish!

Roman advanced on Serge. "You know the alpha told us to treat her with respect. She's the damn reason you're alive!"

Serge scoffed. "She got Lonan killed; she'll get us all killed. She's like a virus, infecting and destroying everything around her."

Roman growled. "That's enough! The alpha will hear about this."

Serge started for the door, his two cronies following him. "The alpha. Wet-behind-the-ears, cursed, and in love with vampires." He threw a hateful glare at Lavinia. "He's another one who should go."

Before any of us could say more, Serge and his friends walked out of the school.

Roman turned to me, his eyes worried. "Are you okay?"

I nodded, my hands still behind my back. "Yeah. It was just ... the same old thing. It's okay."

"No, it's not okay." Roman picked up the two bags he had left beside the door and brought them to the desk. "He should be thankful for you. He should respect you."

I stepped back, afraid my arms were still covered in shadows and he would see them. "I ... I'll be right back."

I zipped out of the office and raced down the hallway, toward the nearest restroom. Once I was safe inside and alone, I looked down at my hands. The shadows were gone.

By the moon, what had that been? Now I could conjure shadows by myself? What the hell was going on with me?

I leaned over the sink and splashed cold water on my face. Moon, I couldn't keep getting into arguments with Serge every day. Besides draining my energy and putting me in a bad mood, I now had to worry about the shadows too.

I was so screwed.

The restroom's door opened and Lavinia spied inside. "May I come in?"

Well, this was a restroom with three sinks and three stalls. Sure she could come in. I sighed. I shouldn't be on the defensive with her.

I nodded. "Sure."

She stepped in and let the door close by itself. "Are you okay?" I opened my mouth to answer, but Lavinia was faster. "And don't lie to me. There's no need for that."

I sighed again. "It's silly. I mean, I just thought that after all we've been through, people would stop stomping on me as if I were a cockroach, you know?"

"I know and I'm sorry," she said.

Lavinia was a pretty vampire-slash-witch with long dark hair and red dyed tips. And unlike all other witches I had met before, she didn't wear the long, fancy gowns. No, she dressed normally, in skinny jeans, a fitted tee or sweater, and boots.

"Sorry. I'm here drowning in self-pity, while I know Serge hasn't been easy on you either." Serge had been a real prick about the vampires, who were there to help. If they were all gone, then his work would increase tenfold and he would still find a way to blame me for all of that.

She rested the side of her hip on one of the sinks. "I don't really care what he thinks." She put a hand to the side of her mouth and whispered, "But that's something new. Before, I would have cared."

I chuckled. "You? You're like badass incarnate."

"Oh, lord, I'm not. What you see, it's mostly a big shift in mindset, and also practice. Before ... I was insecure, and jerks like Serge would have gotten the best of me fast. Besides, I was witch before I was a vampire. Prejudice against witches is a real thing. And I can't even say it's unjust because there are plenty of dark witches out there who tarnish our name."

"I'm sorry."

She shrugged. "We all do the best we can, right?"

"Truer words have never been said."

Her brows knotted. "Raika ... actually, I came in here to check on you, but also, I wanted to talk to you about something."

I tensed. "What is it?"

"I saw the shadows." She stared into my eyes, a gleam of concern in them, and I stood still like a statue, barely breathing. "Right before you hid your hands. I don't think anyone else saw them, not even Serge, who was right there. He was too focused on himself for that, but ... yeah, I saw them. You know about them, don't you?"

I started to deny it, but what was the point? "I don't know what is happening."

"I can sense something in you. I have since we first met."

She narrowed her eyes. "Something dark inside you, something different. I can't pinpoint what it is, but it is there."

That wasn't good. "Lorie and Keeva said the same thing a couple of weeks ago. They said only powerful witches would be able to sense it, but it had always been there. They had noticed before when they had seen me around the pack."

"I know of three kinds of magic that show the same quality," she said. "Dark witches' magic, which manifests in dark color and shadows. Demon magic, which is also like shadows. And shadow fae magic. All of those are similar, but different."

I frowned. "So, you're saying that I have witch, demon, or shadow fae blood in my veins?"

"That, or somehow you tapped into their magics and stole it."

"I've never heard of that before."

"I have, but again, that takes a different species to do that." She pressed a finger to her chin. "If you're curious, what we can do is research. We can start with the library here. I bet there will be books on dark witches, demons, and shadow fae magics. We can see if any of those match yours exactly."

I inhaled sharply. Research it? Find out more? Only if it was on how to keep it hidden. "Hm, no, I don't want to find out more." I walked around her, but paused at the door. "Lavinia, please, don't tell Shane."

She shook her head once, but said, "Okay. This is your secret to tell. I won't say anything."

"Thank you."

I stepped out of the restroom and headed home as if I could leave this entire afternoon inside.

5

RAIKA

WHEN SHANE TEXTED ME SAYING IT WAS TIME FOR OUR RUN, I hesitated.

Looking back, I felt bad for ditching Lavinia, but I wasn't ready to face this. There were so many other things going on. I couldn't wrap my mind around them, let alone something else, something that I had an increasing, sinking feeling wouldn't be a good thing.

I would try to keep this under control until we found the crystals, fixed the barrier, put the town back together, broke Shane's curse. Then, only then, I would tell him about this and figure it out.

Decision made, I put the damn shadow problem out of my mind, took off my clothes, shifted into my wolf, and left my house to meet my mate.

Maybe it was irresponsible of us to be meeting like this when anyone could see us, or when there was so much to be done, but we couldn't work, work, work all the time. We needed to live too.

Where are you, Shane asked in my mind.

Almost there, I told him.

A minute later, I saw him waiting for me at the edge of the forest. I ran to him, but slowed down when I got close. He came to me and brushed his muzzle on mine, like a kiss between wolves. He nudged my shoulder and darted off.

Hey!

I laughed and sprinted after him.

We ran like I had never run before. We weaved through the trees at top speed, jumped over fallen tree limbs, skidded down hills. The rush of the wind over my fur, the zoom of the trees in my ears, the adrenaline pumping in my veins, the company ... it was exhilarating.

Faster, Shane ran circles around me. Once, with the help of a thick tree trunk, he jumped over me in a beautiful arc. It pushed me to run even faster, to try to catch him. But mostly, he slowed down a bit to keep up with me.

It was still fast, and soon we would have made through the entire pack lands surrounding the town. But when we got near the rock formation on the southeast side, Shane guided me toward our place ... the fissure in the rock formation.

We slowed down, and when we were right in front of the fissure, he jumped on me, taking me down. We rolled a bit, until I was lying on the ground—no, not the ground. A thick blanket—and he was on top of me. He lowered his head, brushed it against mine.

Then he shifted.

I shifted too.

In the near darkness of the forest, Shane stared at me with his warm brown eyes, his naked body radiating heat and his scent filling the air. We were both breathing hard, our chests moving fast, and it wasn't just because of the run.

"This wasn't how I imagined the evening going, but it might be even better."

I swallowed. "How did you imagine it?"

"Well, we would run, then we would come here, shift, put on some clothes, make a fire and cook some s'mores and drink wine." He jutted his head to the side. Right at the edge of the blanket was a basket, some folded clothes, and a pile of firewood.

I smiled. "You really thought this evening through."

"I did."

I squirmed under him, aware that his naked body was only a couple of inches from mine. "What else? There's more, isn't there?"

He lowered his head to mine, brushed his lips on mine. "Then I would make my move, kiss you senseless, and make love to you."

Making love to me.

My body tingled with anticipation. "Shane ... just skip most of it and take it from the kiss me senseless part. Now. Please."

He growled before claiming my mouth with his. Painfully slow, he lowered his entire body to mine, and the heat from him, his skin touching mine, it felt too good to be true.

Shane's kiss deepened and I welcomed it. I explored his back with my hands, grazing my nails on the many muscles under his skin. Dear moon, the man had been chiseled out of marble. He was so damn hard.

And that wasn't just his muscles. He moved his body against mine, brushing his hard-on right where I needed him. My body jerked and I gasped against his mouth. I felt his smile before he intensified the kiss and his hand traveled south. He braced himself on one arm, never breaking the kiss, while his other hand found my core. He rubbed his finger over my clit and I gasped, my hands closing around his upper arms.

Deftly, Shane slipped a finger inside me, and at the same time, he moved his mouth from mine, leaving a fiery trail across my cheek, down my neck. His hand started moving, pumping his finger while he played with my clit with his thumb.

Shane lowered his head to my chest and licked the curve of my breast. He went painfully slow, but I knew he was doing it on purpose—I felt like I was going to explode, like it had suddenly become too much for my own skin. He closed his mouth around my breast, sucking on my nipple at the same time he slipped another finger inside me.

My body jerked and I moaned.

This was agony and delight, and everything in between, and I never wanted it to stop.

"By the moon," I whispered. I splayed my hands on the blanket beside us and clutched it, needing some support, something tangible to anchor me to this world, because I was certainly on cloud nine.

Shane thrust his fingers into me, harder, deeper, while his thumb drew circles around my clit, and his tongue played with my nipple.

Dear moon, this was too much. My blood heated, my belly clenched, pure ecstasy traveled through my veins.

"Shane," I whispered.

"Yeah?" he asked before closing his mouth over my breast again.

I was a goner.

I cried as I came, my body trembling uncontrollably. I flew through cloud nine as the sensation lessened. Shane watched me as he moved fully on top of me, one corner of his lips tugged up. He brought his fingers to his mouth and tasted me.

"Delicious. Next time, I'll do it with my mouth again."

Oh, moon, again. We would do this again. Yes, please. All the time. Forever.

I hooked my legs around his waist and pulled him to me. "Come here," I muttered, breathless.

Shane braced both arms on either side of my shoulder, staring at me. His hard-on brushed against my entrance. "Do you want this?" I tugged my feet at his ass, showing it instead of answering. "You have to tell me. I won't go further before you say it."

"Dear moon, yes, I want it. I want you. Inside me. Now. Please."

He showed me that lopsided smile before lowering himself to me and brushing his lips on mine. Slowly, he slipped inside me.

"Oh," I whispered as his length stretched my walls and I tensed.

Shane stilled and stared back at me. "You're a virgin?"

"Yeah. What did you expect?"

His eyes darkened. "I ... You're so pretty, so hot. I thought someone else had tried getting in your pants before."

"No one wanted to get in the omega's pants."

A growl started in his chest. "Let me just tell you, knowing this is your first time, that you're only mine, it's so fucking hot."

He pressed his mouth to mine and kissed me slowly but hard. Matching the kiss, he moved again, sliding inside me, filling me with his massive erection. When I thought I would explode, that my core would rip apart, he stopped again, giving my body time to adjust to him.

Moon, he was big and hard, and I wanted him, all of him. "Move," I whispered against his mouth.

"My damn pleasure." He clasped my nape and kissed me as he started moving, dragging himself in and out of me, slowly at first, the friction turning my brain into mush.

But with each passing minute, Shane thrust faster and harder and deeper, until my veins were at boiling point again.

Shane broke the kiss and whispered in my ear, "I have a confession. I haven't done this in years, and none of those other times compared to this. To you. I won't last long."

"Then don't." I clutched his arms, tightened my legs around his waist, and tugged him to me. "Just keep going."

He groaned and buried his face in my neck. His lips brushed my skin, sending shivers racing down my spine. That mixed with the fire building inside me, it was the ingredient for combustion.

I felt it as Shane sped up, my belly clenching, my toes curling, the tingling sensation in my veins. I was close, so damn close.

Shane grazed his teeth on my neck and I gasped with the sensation. He dragged his mouth to mine again, kissing me as hard and deep as he was moving inside me.

I tried holding it, to make it last longer, but there was no use. I burst into a million pleasure pieces in Shane's arms. Three seconds later, he groaned, his body tensed, and then broke out in little trembles.

He kissed me as he rode down his ecstasy, his hot body weighing over mine. When the tremors were gone, he pulled back and stared into my eyes, a soft smile on his lips.

"We should probably move on to the part of my plan we skipped earlier."

I chuckled. "I like that idea."

WE DIDN'T PUT on the clothes Shane had brought. Instead, we grabbed the extra blanket, wrapped ourselves in it, with me seated in front of Shane, my back to his chest, his legs in crisscross applesauce under my ass, and his arms around me.

I had never imagined a moment like this, with Shane or anyone else, and it baffled my mind. Being here, like this, with him, holding sticks with our marshmallows over the small campfire he had lit, was amazing. I could stay like this forever.

Well, we could definitely alternate between having sex and snuggling like this with s'mores. It would be even more perfect and even the faint pain I felt from my first time couldn't ruin that.

I glanced around the flames from the fire casting moving shadows over the trees and the fissure in the rock formation. I could hear crickets, and an owl in the distance.

Otherwise, it was just us.

"How did you manage this?" I asked. My marshmallow turned golden and I pressed the chocolate and crackers around it. "Aren't wolves and vampires scouting the forest?"

Shane nodded, his chin brushing on the back of my head. I took a bite of my s'mores and turned slightly to look at him. "They are, but tonight, I told them to avoid this area. No explanation needed."

"No one seemed curious?"

"They sure did." Shane's marshmallow was black by the

time he took it out of the fire. The way he liked it. Go figure. He assembled his s'more. "But I didn't care. Though, of course, Killian knows about this outing. Lavinia too. I had to make sure someone knew where to find me, just in case. They've known about us for a while now, and I trust them."

With my mouth full, I nodded. I swallowed. "They seem like good people. Or vampires."

"They are. I owe them a lot for rescuing me, and here they are helping me still." He took a big bite of his s'more.

"That's what good friends are for, isn't it? Or so I've heard." I had never had any real friends, other than my mother, Rue, and Minsi. Maybe Roman could be considered a friend. But they weren't my age or my peers. Besides them, I had had no one.

Shane swallowed and frowned. "Lavinia told me Serge gave you a hard time this afternoon."

I tensed. Had she kept her word and not told him what had happened? "Hm, yeah." I shrugged, waiting for him to ask me more about it, about the shadows. I waited a few seconds, but he didn't say anything. "I don't think we should bother with him. He won't change, no matter what we do."

"When I promote your rank, he'll have to respect you."

"But that won't be true respect. It'll be forced, and he will hate me even more." I ate the rest of my s'more, chewed, swallowed. "I've been thinking about the ranking thing. When you promote me, won't someone else become the omega?"

"I've been thinking about that too. I'm trying to devise a system where there's no omega. Maybe the alpha, the betas, the warriors, and then the rest of the wolves have the same rank. No one needs to be at the bottom."

"Can you do that? Isn't that something innate to wolves? There always has to be an omega."

"I don't know. That's what I'm trying to find out. Maybe we'll need Lavinia's help to make a new ranking system work?" He shrugged and put the last of his s'mores in his mouth. We had already eaten about five each. I felt full and sweetened all over.

"Who was omega before my family?" I asked. I had never considered this.

"Roman's father's family."

My eyes rounded. "Really? He never said anything."

"I guess once someone finally digs themselves up from that position, they don't want to talk about it."

"It isn't that bad," I said, on the defensive. Shane lifted an eyebrow at me. "Okay. It was. It is."

"Raika, I want to tell you why your family was demoted to omega."

My gut clenched. "I changed my mind about that. Maybe I don't want to know."

Shane shook his head. "It's not bad. Look, when they were teenagers, my father loved your mother."

"What?"

"Yeah, he thought that they would be mates, but your mother wasn't into him. They had a couple of dates and then she was done with him."

"I can't blame her, he was a damn jerk." I flinched at my words. "Sorry."

"No, you're right, he was. And he was also proud and stubborn. When your mother said she wouldn't go out with him anymore, when he insisted and she kept turning him down, he demoted your family to omega. As punishment."

I gaped at him. "Are you serious?"

He nodded. "My mother told me and your mother told her."

Wow, one surprising punch after the other. This was not going the way I thought it would. "What? Your mother talked to my mother?"

"My mother was kind and had a big heart. Did you know she admired you? She really did." That brought some heat to my cheeks. "And because of you and your hardworking mother, she wanted to see what she could do for you. So since my father wouldn't tell her what happened, she talked to your mother and your mother told her. My mother confronted my father about it, and he admitted it. Because your mother turned him down, he demoted her entire family to omega."

"Wow ... and my mother wasn't even his mate."

"Right. He demoted your family before meeting my mother and mating with her. What I hate the most is that even though he had found out he had been wrong about your mother, he didn't undo his mistake. He let your family be the omega because he was a bastard."

I took a moment to process that information. So ... the truth about our demotion was a lot less dire than I thought it would be. It had been because Franc hadn't gotten his way. And what would have happened if my mother had liked him, had dated him, and then he found his mate? He would have left her, heartbroken and alone.

But we probably wouldn't be the omegas.

There were so many wrong things with this.

"I'm sorry," Shane said, his voice low. He rubbed his hand on my bare arm under the blanket. "I didn't want to tell you before because it's so stupid, it doesn't make any sense. But I also didn't want any more secrets hanging over our heads. You deserve the truth, always."

Ouch.

Way to make me feel guilty. Because I had a big secret and I didn't want to tell him yet. Because I had no idea what this secret meant, why I could move the shadows, why I could control them in certain situations. Because we had too much on our plates already.

Because I was afraid of myself. I didn't want other people afraid of me. I couldn't handle it.

I swallowed hard, trying to get past it all.

"You understand now why I want to promote your rank? Because it was unjust, because you deserve better."

I nodded, but I didn't agree. Right now, I felt like I didn't deserve anything.

I fell silent as I staked another marshmallow and placed it over the fire. I wasn't hungry anymore, but I needed to do something with my hands, occupy my mind.

"How's the search for the crystals and the witches going?"

Shane groaned. "Not well. We killed most of the Night-mist witches last year."

"And now Lorie and Keeva are dead too."

"I had to kill them. I was using my curse as my plan B. If they saw me, they would have told Conri about it, and then the element of surprise would be gone."

I nodded. "The ones who are left are probably hiding."

"Right. As for Dixon and the crystals, every trail the vampires find goes cold. It's like he's playing with us. And what I can't stop thinking is, what if he doesn't have the crystals anymore? What if he sold them to someone more powerful? What if he used them, drained them of their magic? We're chasing him, but what if we find him and the crystals are gone?"

"You can't think like that." I placed the stick and the marshmallow down, letting it burn completely. I turned a little more and looked at Shane. "You have to have faith. And maybe ... we need to think of a plan B. Didn't you say Lavinia tried contacting the original witch coven who spelled the pack lands and gave us the crystals?"

"She did, but we don't even know the name of the coven."

"We can continue looking for them, even without a name. There are plenty of older supernaturals in this world and libraries filled with books about our kinds. Someone is bound to know something that will lead us to them." I considered. "And we can come up with a plan C too."

"Plan C?"

"Yeah. What about if we get all these powerful witches you know and they come here to recreate the first spell. We find two new crystals, or if that doesn't work, we find four new crystals and redo everything."

Shane stared at the crackling fire for a moment. "That isn't a bad idea."

I smiled at him. "I'm not too bad."

He chuckled. "You're not bad at all." He snaked his arm around my waist and pressed his mouth to mine. "By the way, you lied before."

"I did?" My eyes bugged. Was he talking the shadows now? "About what?"

"That no one wanted to get into the omega's pants." He lifted his index finger. "You couldn't have known, but I did. I really did." I rolled my eyes. He raised his middle finger. "And Roman. He wanted to get into your pants since you were a teenager and he still wants to."

I narrowed my eyes at him. "Do I hear jealousy in your voice?"

"No!" he said quickly. "I mean, I'm your mate, you're here with me, aren't you? But still, I don't like the way he looks at you. I can't wait until we can tell everyone you're mine."

"Do you want to talk about the way Roman looks at me. How about how Lucille looks at you? The way she touches you, bats her eyelashes at you, the way she brings you lunch … I would do that if people wouldn't be suspicious."

"Now who's jealous?" I punched his shoulder and he laughed. "I kind of like you jealous. Maybe I should spend more time with Lucille and—"

I punched him again. "Don't you dare."

Growing serious, Shane cupped my face. "Don't be jealous of her. She's barely my friend now. You're the one I want. You're my mate and nothing will change that."

He pressed his mouth to mine. I parted my lips to him and let him kiss me, just as breathlessly as he always did. I would never get used to how good this felt, to the deep, warm feeling in my chest tugging me toward him.

I felt as his desire manifested itself under me.

Emboldened, I took control of the kiss, of the entire situation. Without breaking the kiss, I spun on his lap and straddled him. I held on to his shoulders as I adjusted myself and slipped him inside me.

I moaned against his mouth as he filled me, as the delicious sensation began anew, and the fire burned inside me.

"Holy shit," he whispered, clasping my waist and changing his legs position.

I started moving. Up and down, taking him deeper and deeper. I pulled back and stared at him, at this handsome man under me, at how his mouth was parted, at how he stared at me with such desire in his eyes, how he groaned every time I pushed down until he was buried inside me.

I stared back at him, such a powerful energy passing

between our gazes, and I kept moving, faster and faster. I opened my knees a little more, and somehow he went even deeper. A delicious shiver ran down my spine.

"Raika," he said with a growl. "This is so fucking good."

"I know." I leaned back, and dear moon, that took us even deeper. The friction was too much. His glistening naked body was too much. His intense stare was too much.

I wanted to drown in this sensation.

With a cry, I came. My body broke out in tremors and I did my best not to stop moving, but I lost to the ecstasy. Shane's hands around my waist tightened and he moved his hips up to meet mine, and each time he did, I trembled again, my climax renewed.

Then he encircled his arm like a vice around my waist and buried his head on my chest as he climaxed. He held me tight against him until his tremors faded.

I stayed right there, not willing to move from above him, to unglue my body from his.

Shane looked at me. He brushed my hair back from my sweaty face. He fixed his intense gaze on mine. "I don't want to scare you, I know you're just getting used to this mating thing, and to me, but I need you to know ... I love you."

My chest tightened with a dozen unspoken feelings. "I love you too," I whispered, and it was the damn truth. I knew half of this was the mating bond's doing, but the other half was us, him. Shane was turning out to be a great alpha and I was proud of him.

I really did love him.

Shane's smile brightened and he embraced me, his arms tight around me.

6

SHANE

I ALMOST SPENT THE REST OF THE NIGHT WITH RAIKA AT HER house. I really wanted to, but I was worried about Minsi. What if she had a panic attack and I wasn't there? I knew Rue could handle her, Raika had taught her how, but I didn't like the idea of Minsi going through that while I was enjoying myself.

I probably should have been worried about Rue finding out about Raika and me, but I didn't. One, because I thought Rue had already put two and two together. She had seen Raika and me around each other many times, more than most wolves, and she wasn't stupid. I was out now doing what? Working? Maybe. Possibly. But she was wise. She knew I was with someone, and that someone could only be Raika.

Truth was, I wasn't worried about anyone finding out about Raika and me. I was damn proud of being her mate; I wanted to shout it out for everyone to hear. But I agreed with Raika. Things were wobbly. We couldn't add gasoline to the fire.

But every time I said good night to Raika, it hurt more and

more. I was incredibly satisfied and happy we had made love —finally! I had been pining over her for so damn long. But I wanted more. I wanted to cook for her, to spy as she got dressed in the mornings, to brush my teeth while she took a shower, to hold her in my sleep.

By the moon, I couldn't wait to have her under me again ... above me too. A thrill ran through me thinking ... she was mine, only mine. There were plenty of other positions and things for us to explore, and I couldn't wait.

I adjusted the sudden bulk in my pants and shook my head as I got the mug from under the coffee pot. The sun wasn't up yet. I had slept for a measly few hours, but I was in a good mood. I sounded like a freaking sap and I couldn't say I hated it. But it was funny. Though I had been into Raika and dreamed about her for years, I hadn't thought beyond just winning her over. I never thought I would feel this way about anyone, that I would want the whole nine yards. And I knew I only wanted it because it was with her.

I heard Tyren coming down the stairs and frowned. When he entered the kitchen from the mudroom, I asked, "What are you doing up so early?"

"Wolf ears." He pointed to his right ear. "You might think you're being careful with sounds, but you're not."

"Your sister didn't wake up."

"I went to sleep late and—"

"You were playing video games."

"That's not what we're discussing here."

So there was a discussion here. I leaned on the kitchen counter and stared at him. "What are we discussing?"

"I heard you coming in late last night. Where were you?"

"I'm twenty-two. The damn alpha of this pack. I don't need to answer to you."

Tyren's face closed up. "You're a parental figure for Minsi and me. You're our only family. You can't go around, searching for crystals or witches to—"

I crossed the kitchen and wrapped my arms around him. Tyren was almost as tall as I was, but a lot slimmer—with the right workout, he would get there. I thought it would feel odd to embrace him like this, but damn it, he was my little brother. He had been locked in a classroom with one meal per day for a year. He saw our parents killed; he thought I had left them, *him*, behind.

He was afraid it was going to happen again.

Tyren stiffened at first, but after three seconds, he patted my back hard.

"I'm not going anywhere. I promise, I'll be careful. You and Minsi are the most important thing to me." And Raika too. "I'll do everything I can to keep you safe."

Tyren pushed away from me, his nose wrinkled. "Never mind what I said. I see now you were out on a mission."

"What do you mean?"

"I smell Raika all over you."

I gaped at him. Shit, I hadn't considered that. "I ... Hm ..."

"Save it. I know you like her, and she likes you too." He opened the kitchen cabinet and picked up an empty mug. "So is this for fun, or what? Is she your mate?"

My jaw opened, closed. I shouldn't lie to him. "She's my mate."

Nodding, Tyren turned the coffeemaker back on. "I approve."

I scoffed. I didn't need his approval. But it was good to hear. "Thanks."

"That's why you're promoting her rank?"

"The moment she became my mate, her rank changed.

And when I became alpha, it changed again. Theoretically, she's the highest-ranking female in the pack."

"True." He pressed a button on the coffeemaker and it rumbled to life. "So, that means, Lucille is free?"

I shook my head. "Tyren, Lucille is twenty-one, six years older than you. Right now, she probably considers you a younger brother. If you're really into her, wait another five or ten years to try something, okay?"

He shrugged. "No promises."

I cocked my head, taking a good look at him. "Raika told me you were like a moody teenager most of the time while in … while I was away. And you are, most of the time since the pack was freed, but right now, you're different. What's going on?"

"Nothing." He rolled his eyes. "Okay. I had a conversation with Killian yesterday after practice. I was complaining you were treating me like a kid, and he said that might be because I was acting like one, especially when around you. He said I should try to be more like your friend. Then maybe you would trust me and let me help more."

By the moon, I had to have a talk with Killian. Or not. I didn't like the idea of Tyren in the battlefield, but this interaction we were having was nice. I could easily see the both of us enjoying spending time together if it was always like this.

"Killian is an old vampire. You know what they say, wisdom comes with age."

Tyren half-smiled, something I did often. "And when are you going to be wise? When you're two hundred years old?"

Two hundred for a wolf was like ninety for a human.

I shook my head. "Just … eat your breakfast and get ready. Today you'll be accompanying me everywhere."

Tyren's eyes rounded. "Are you serious?"

"Yeah. I'm alpha, but if something were to happen to me, you're next in line. You have to learn how to take care of the pack." Not that I knew what I was doing. I had studied with our father for many years, but it was one thing reading records and watching from the sides. Another was actually being at the helm and navigating a stormy sea with a ship full of holes.

His brows slammed down. "I don't want to be alpha. You will live long, and one day, one of your pups with Raika will be your successor."

Pups with Raika. Even though I wasn't ready to be a father, I liked that picture for the future. "That's okay. But we never know what tomorrow is going to be like." I drank the rest of my not-so-hot coffee. "Get ready. We leave in fifteen."

TYREN DIDN'T COMPLAIN, even when I noticed his breathing came in faster bursts in the middle of morning practice. He had run the perimeter of the pack lands with me, and he helped lead the practice with the other wolves.

The others saw how I coached Tyren, and the older ones took note of what was happening. I was grooming a successor in case something happened to me. Serge was the first to voice his displeasure.

I was already enraged because he bullied Raika yesterday. I didn't hold it in. I sent the old wolf to run four laps around the pack lands, and if he slowed or stopped, he had to start over.

He called me names under his breath as he turned, shifted, and dashed away.

If he continued provoking me like this, I would have to do more than punish him with laps.

After practice, Tyren and I went to my office at town hall. Lavinia had said she would bring lunch to all of us, but Lucille came in with a big sandwich for me and for Tyren. She halted by the door and watched us as we took bites of our lunch.

"Is it good?" she asked with a smile.

"Delicious," Tyren said, his mouth full. He stared at her like a damn puppy.

I swallowed and said, "Thank you, Lucille, but you know you don't need to do this."

"I know, but it's the least I can do." Her smile dimmed. "Oh, Shane, I actually came with a request today."

This couldn't be good. "What is it?"

"You know, during both battles ... some females fought because we were right there, but we didn't really know what we were doing. We had fighting lessons while in school, but after that, your father never allowed females to train with the male wolves."

I nodded. My father was old-fashioned that way. Nowadays, women wanted to be involved in everything, which I thought was fair.

"Let me guess, you want to train with us?"

"Not just me. I talked to Celina, Jena, and Raika. We all want to train."

My heart tugged. Raika wanted to train? Like Tyren, I didn't like the idea of her in a fight, but she had been in fights before. And despite not being trained properly, she had done well. Imagine if she could fight. She would kick some serious ass.

"I like that idea."

Lucille gasped. "You do? Are you serious?"

I nodded. "Yes. The four of you can join us for practice tomorrow."

She clapped her hands, excited. "I'll let the others know right away." She ran out of my office.

Tyren glared at me. "Females fighting?"

"Why not? Like Lucille said, they had some basic training in school and I remember many of them being rather good. If they continued training, they could be as good as us. And the moon knows we need all the help we can get."

He leaned closer and whispered, "Aren't you worried about Raika getting hurt?"

I clenched my teeth, unclenched them. "Yes, I am, but she already showed all of us that she can protect herself, and all of us too."

Tyren let out a long sigh. "You're the alpha. I won't argue with you."

"Good." I took another bite of my sandwich.

A minute later, Lavinia and Killian came into the office, carrying disposable lunch boxes.

"Oh." Lavinia stared at us. "Let me guess, Lucille?"

"Bingo," I said between bites.

She rolled her eyes. "You've got to set her straight."

"And what will I say to her? Lucille, I appreciate your attention, but I'm in love with someone else."

Killian pointed at Tyren.

I nodded. "He knows."

"If you do that, she'll ask who, and it won't take her three seconds to realize who," Lavinia said. She placed the lunch boxes on my desk. "And then the real problem begins."

"Why?" Tyren asked. "Why aren't you telling anyone?"

I explained to him all the reasoning about it. Despite

wanting to tell everyone about so I could walk around with Raika's hand in mine, as I said it all out loud, I once more realized it made sense to wait.

Tyren nodded and shoved the last piece of his sandwich in his mouth. Lavinia and Killian leaned against the low filing cabinet to the side and started eating their lunch of carbonara pasta—made by Rue, no doubt. Her cooking skills were legendary. I regretted eating the sandwich now.

Killian's phone rang. He picked it up, looked at screen, and frowned. "It's Taos." Taos was one of the vampires he had sent to search for the crystals. "He wasn't supposed to call me until later this evening to report." Killian answered the call. "Taos, what happened?"

I focused my wolf hearing on the conversation.

"We've found him," Taos said. My eyebrows lifted. "He seems to be hiding in a luxurious hotel in Calgary." That was one state over, in Alberta. "So far, he seems to be alone, but earlier this morning, he went into an abandoned farm outside of town. We couldn't get close. It was full of demons."

"Does he have the crystals?" Killian asked.

"I haven't seen them, but he carried something in the inside pockets of his jacket. He keeps checking the items to see if they are still there."

Would he be carrying the crystal with him, or would he have hidden them somewhere safe? What would I have done? I would probably have hidden them, but who said these demons were smart?

I couldn't risk letting him go without knowing.

"Tell him to keep an eye on Dixon. Trail his every move, and if he leaves, follow him. We'll be there by tomorrow afternoon." I stood up. "Time to gear up."

7

RAIKA

Dom had gone to the nearest town and gotten the computers, laptops, tablets, and phones from our place there. He had brought it all in the back of his pickup truck and parked in front of the library.

"Special delivery," he told me as he entered the library.

The next few minutes I spent cataloging everything in the truck. Meanwhile, a line formed on the sidewalk as people realized their new electronics had arrived. Lucille and Roman helped me distribute those to our people, and then to take other desktops and laptops to the town hall, infirmary, school, library, and all other important buildings in town.

We had also bought tablets for the school. Each kid would have their own tablet in school, where they could do special activities and play educational games. I hoped they liked them.

I couldn't wait for the kids to return to regular school soon. Maybe it seemed silly to worry about that when there were so many other things to do around town, and it was almost summer, when usually there was a bigger break from classes, but when talking to Shane, Rue, and Vianna about this, they all agreed with me that we needed to give something for the kids to do while the adults worried about the other things. They needed their minds and hands occupied, and what better way than school? Besides, they had already spent a year locked away, unable to read or play. They were eager to go back to a real school.

But since the school had also been their prison, I was working hard to paint the walls and change things, so they wouldn't easily remember what transpired here.

I spent my afternoon hooking up computers, turning them on, setting them up, first in the school, then at the library. I hadn't been ten minutes inside the library, when Rue brought Minsi over.

"She insisted on coming," she said. "The others want to go play at the lake."

Minsi stayed with me while I worked, but I knew I didn't need to worry about her. The girl picked up a book, settled down on the rug in the middle of the library, and lost herself in fantasy worlds.

Though I wished she would have gone to play with the other kids, I was glad she was out of trouble and doing what she liked, where she liked—that meant fewer panic attacks.

I was behind the front desk, fighting with some stupid cables that didn't reach to the damn outlet, when I felt it. I couldn't explain it, maybe it was the bond, but when I turned around, I knew who I would see: Shane in the doorway to the backroom.

He smiled at me and butterflies took off in my stomach.

As I walked to him, memories of last night flooded my mind and my cheeks heated. I had done such a great job of keeping him out of my mind today and focusing on my work.

But here and there, an image came back, a sensation hit me again, and I smiled.

Last night had been amazing, like nothing I could have ever imagined, and even though I knew nights like that one wouldn't happen too often for the foreseeable future, the prospect that someday spending my nights with Shane would be the norm thrilled me.

I joined him in the backroom. "What are you doing here?" I asked in a low voice.

Shane didn't answer. No. He simply clasped a hand around the nape of my neck, wound his other arm around my waist, and pulled me to him. His mouth crashed on mine, and I moaned as my body came alive and demanded more.

I would have kissed him forever if his sister wasn't in the other room. She was a sneaky one, known to go from room to room quiet as a mouse. I gently broke the kiss, but stayed in his arms, right where I liked it.

"Hey, everything okay? You usually don't visit me during the day like this." Because it was risky.

Shane rested his forehead on mine. "I've missed you."

I chuckled. "It has been only, what, a few hours?" I teased, but the truth was, I also missed him.

"Fifteen hours, give or take, but who is counting?"

I gaped at him. He had been counting?

He shrugged. "We parted around midnight, and it's the middle of the afternoon. A simple calculation."

I shook my head. "You're incorrigible."

"But you like it."

Yes. Yes, I did. I smoothed my hands over his shoulders. I really liked touching him. "As much as I like this visit, I know something is up."

He nodded. "Dixon was found."

I blinked. "What? Where?"

"In Calgary. We're leaving tonight. Hopefully, we'll arrive there by tomorrow morning."

I stepped back from him. "Okay, I need to get my things and—"

"Raika," Shane started. "I want to ask you to stay." I stared at him, at a loss for words. "I want you to come. I know you want to come, but—"

I lifted a finger. "Don't give me the it's-too-dangerous bullshit."

"No, it's not that. I swear." He raised both his hands, palms out. "I think you're more than capable of protecting yourself and kicking some ass, but that's not it. I want you to stay to watch over Minsi, Tyren, and the rest of the pack." That ... wasn't what I was expecting. "There's no one I trust more than you, and I know you care about this pack even more than I do. If something happens to me—"

"Don't go there."

"We don't know how this will go or how long it'll take. Dom is coming with me. Vallin is staying, and I know he'll keep an eye on everyone, but it's not the same. If you stay, I know our pack will be fine. And if something happens to me, you can reveal what you are to me and help Tyren become the next alpha. You can help him lead the pack until he's mature enough."

I shook my head and took a step back. "We're so not having this conversation."

Shane reached for me. He took my hand in his. "I'm asking you as your mate to stay and watch over my siblings and our pack."

My chest hurt. Why was he doing this to me? I would rather he had treated this like a quick pick-up service. As if he was going into the nearest town to retrieve the stuff we had bought and would be back soon.

But here he was, taking this thing to a whole new level. Because he wasn't going on a pick-up run, he was going after a demon who had helped Conri while we were his slaves. A demon who could have used the crystals to make him stronger, who could have allies out there, who could give us a run for our money.

I hated this. But I understood Shane's position. As alpha, he had to think of more, of all of us. He had to think about the future. I blew out a breath. "All right. I'll stay. But with one condition. You keep me informed. I want a text every two minutes."

A half smile tugged at his lips. "I promise." He pulled me back to him and I didn't resist it. My body molded to his and a pang cut through my chest. I didn't want him to go, but I knew he had to. "We're leaving tonight and I'm not sure I'll be able to sneak to see you again before that."

He would probably be surrounded by his betas and the other wolves and vampires who would accompany him, and most of them didn't know about us.

"Just ... be careful. Please."

He pressed his lips to my forehead. "I will."

Shane and the others left early in the evening. I didn't see him again, but he sent me a text to let me know.

After taking a shower, I packed a small bag and went to his house.

It was eight in the evening when I made my way to Shane's house, and it was still bright outside. I knew this was normal for this time of the year, but we weren't used to this.

A few clouds dotted the sky and a breeze blew a little chillier than before. The change in temperature since the barrier went down was jarring. I couldn't imagine how it would be when winter arrived.

Hopefully, Shane would come back tomorrow with the crystals and the barrier would come back, protecting us once again.

I was enjoying my quiet walk, until of course, it wasn't quiet anymore.

Serge's house was on the way and he was on the porch with his friends, drinking beer and playing cards.

The moment he saw me, he stood and leaned over the porch rails. "Are you going to the alpha's house to work, whore? Isn't it too early for you? Oh wait, he isn't here, is he?"

"Tyren is there, though," Buck said, his words lost between laughter.

Serge guffawed. "Right! The whore will work tonight after all."

Ew. My stomach knotted. Tyren was fifteen, by the moon. They didn't even respect the alpha's younger brother? They were disgusting.

Chin high, I kept walking, as if they didn't exist.

"Hey, where do you think you're going, whore?" one of them shouted.

"Come back here," Serge yelled. "We could use your services."

By the moon ...

I sped up, wishing I could scrub my ears clean.

"Hey," someone said from behind me and I jumped. Roman fell into step with me. "It's me, sorry."

I pressed a hand to my chest. "Holy shit, Roman, do you want to give me a heart attack?"

"Sorry. I thought you could hear me."

I shook my head. "No, I was too focused on getting away from those creeps."

"I heard them. I wanted to make sure they didn't follow you."

I frowned. "If they try something, they'll be sorry."

"I know you can handle yourself, but it doesn't matter. I feel better knowing you're safe."

I frowned. Would now be a good time to let him down nicely? I hated the idea of hurting him, but dragging this along was even worse.

"Roman, I—"

"I heard Shane got a group together and is going after the crystals," he said. If he had interrupted me on purpose or if he hadn't heard me, I didn't know. "And he asked you to stay with his brother and sister."

"Yeah, hm, who told you that?"

"Actually, I heard it. I was walking by Lucille and Dom right before he left with Shane. She was complaining she hadn't been invited to go, and that he hadn't asked her to watch his siblings either. That he had asked you."

"Because of Minsi," I added quickly.

"Yeah, Dom told her that. You know how to deal with Minsi in case she has one of her attacks. Lucille didn't seem happy anyway."

The alpha's house came into view from Main Street. "There's nothing I can do about that."

"I know."

I turned into the house's long driveway. "Thanks for the company."

Roman opened his mouth, his brows curled down, but then he shook his head. "Good night, Raika."

I waved at him and made my way to the front door before he changed his mind and said whatever he was going to say. I felt like a coward for not having the courage to set him free.

At some point, I would have to do it.

I waited until he walked away to use my key—the moon forbid he might see I had my own keys—to unlock the front door and enter the house.

Once I stepped in, Minsi shot from the couch, dropped her book, and ran for me. Tyren, who was watching an action movie on the big flat screen, raised his hand and said, "Hey."

I hugged Minsi back. "Hey, pretty girl. Did you already have dinner?" She shook her head. "All right, then let's cook something." I offered her my hand, she took it, and together, we walked into the kitchen.

I made them a rice and chicken baked casserole, and even Tyren took thirds, and asked me if I could come cook dinner for them every night.

One day. Maybe one day, in the near future, I would.

8

SHANE

When Taos said Dixon was hiding in a fancy hotel, he wasn't kidding. The hotel was close to downtown Calgary, and it had valets and bellmen with white gloves, a red carpet at the entrance, and so far, we had seen at least three Porsches and two Ferraris stop in the curved driveaway. The front was glass with golden pillars and we could see the luxurious reception with plenty of velvet couches, tall statues, giant flower arrangements, and guests dressed in their finest.

"Why would a demon hide in a hotel like this?" Dom asked from my right.

We were at a coffeeshop across the street, sitting at three different tables, all of us with laptops or books, as if we were working. Though we didn't know what we would find, I thought a large group would only make things more difficult to coordinate, so I had only brought Killian, Lavinia, and Dom. We had met with Taos and earlier that morning when we arrived in town.

"Hide in plain sight?" I suggested. It was my only train of thought. Why hide in a shitty inn in a small town, when you can lose yourself in a big city? I adjusted the baseball cap I had donned for this mission. "It isn't a bad idea."

"Taos, you said he came in late last night?" Killian asked. "And hasn't left yet?"

Taos shook his head. "Louis has been stationed at the back entrance since then and so far, none of us has seen him leaving."

"We swept the hotel yesterday," Kalon said. "There's only another entrance to the side, but it spills there." He pointed to a narrow alley between the hotel and the building beside it. "Or to the back. Either way, we would have seen it."

"Unless he turned into a bat and flew from here," Dom joked. Lavinia chuckled and Killian rolled his eyes. "What? That was funny."

I shook my head. It was almost noon. We had been here since sunrise. He either had seen us and wasn't leaving because of that, or he had already left, somehow. We couldn't waste the day away here.

"All right," I said. "We'll wait for another hour. If he doesn't show, Killian and Lavinia will go in the hotel and search for him. If he's in there, flush him out. Taos will go with Dom to the farm outside of town, to see if he's there. Either way—"

I shut my mouth when a man stepped out of the hotel.

Dixon.

He wore a long black jacket with the large collar turned up, hiding half of his face. He halted at the entrance and glanced side to side.

"We should get him now," Dom suggested.

"We're too exposed here." If wolf shifters and vampires attacked a demon in daylight in the middle of a big city, it would be chaos. "Let's follow him. Dom, discreetly get the car ready."

He nodded, closed his book and notepad, put them inside his bag, and walked away.

A minute later, a red Mustang stopped in front of Dixon. A valet stepped out and held the door open for him. Dixon didn't acknowledge the valet as he entered his car. He drove away fast.

We shot up, grabbed our things, and ran to the cars.

Dom had our black SUV ready, with the doors open in the coffeeshop's side parking lot. We jumped inside—me in the passenger seat, Killian and Lavinia in the third row, Taos and Kalon in the second row.

"Go," I said as soon as everyone hopped in.

Dom stepped on it and we chased after the red Mustang. In three blocks, we caught up with Dixon. Behind us, a silver sedan appeared. Louis.

We maintained a healthy distance from the Mustang, and when he left the town and traffic was almost nonexistent, we let him go. Taos told us he was on the way to the farm and he knew how to get there.

Of course, that didn't mean Dixon couldn't have changed routes or go somewhere else, but I was willing to see how it panned out.

We parked the SUV and the sedan a good mile from the farm. We walked the rest of the way, through the neighboring land, with our eyes and ears always open for patrols.

But there was nothing.

We approached the farm. Weathered boards danged from the roof of the barn, and the doors flapped in the wind. A handful of cars were parked in the back, including a red Mustang.

"How many demons have you seen?" I asked the vampires.

"A little over a dozen," Taos said as we crouched behind a wooden fence covered with dying vines. "But we think there are more inside."

If it was two dozen, then our odds were three to one. Doable, if we could use the element of surprise.

"What do you want to do?" Dom asked me.

I wanted to wait for night, so we could use the darkness to our advantage, but Dixon could leave until then, and only the moon knew where he could go next. Go back into town in the middle of humans? Or somewhere with even more demons? We couldn't risk it.

"Surround the barn," I said. "On my signal, we rush in and attack. Kill everyone, if necessary. But if Dixon doesn't have the crystals, keep him alive. We'll need him to find out what he did with them."

The others nodded in agreement and started rounding the barn, keeping a good distance so as not to alert the demons.

I waited until everyone was in position, took off my clothes, chucked them aside, and shifted into my wolf form.

Ready? I asked Dom.

Ready, he said through our mental link.

Let's do this.

I jumped from behind the fence and Dom followed my lead. The vampires saw us moving and dashed after us. Because they were faster than us, they slowed down so the seven of us burst into the barn at the same time.

The demons stood still for two seconds, taking in as we surrounded them in the large, practically empty barn. Dixon leaned over a long table in the center, and the other demons stood around him.

"What is this?" a demon asked. He changed, his skin darkening and thickening, hidden horns losing their glamour.

Following his lead, all the demons changed into their true forms, each one more hideous than the others.

"Kill them," was all Dixon said.

We charged the demons before they could.

I jumped over one, who tumbled over another one. I bit down the throat of the first one, and pawed the second's one face. He cried out and tried moving from underneath us, but when he was finally able to scoot a few inches away, I was already on top of him. I closed my mouth around his shoulder and ripped it open.

The demon cried as blood oozed out.

I turned to a third demon. This one threw his shadow magic at me, but I dodged in. A fourth demon rammed into me my side. I swiped my paw at him, momentarily distracting him. The third demon threw more of his magic at me, but I twisted, taking the fourth demon with me and using him as a shield. The fourth demon cried as the shadow hit his back. I silenced him by ripping his throat out.

Jumping over his fallen body, I went directly for the fourth's neck.

I turned to a fifth one, but a second later, he fell right in front of me. I glanced around and saw I hadn't been the only one to leave a trail of bodies.

The few demons left were engaged in fights against my friends, and I knew they could handle those. So, I turned to Dixon, who was in the same exact place since we entered the barn, though now, he had his back to the table and watched me.

"You'll never have them." He kicked a black box under the table. "I'll kill all of you before I let you have it."

The demon was sorely mistaken. What chance did he have against three wolf shifters and five vampires? Impatient, I lunged at him. Dixon was the ugliest demon of all with a sickly gray-brown skin, short arms, thick legs, and a long, scaly tail.

He snapped his teeth in the air, but I swiped my paw at his big head and threw him to the ground. I went for his neck, but he punched my gut and rolled from underneath me.

I turned to him, but I didn't need to worry. Killian and Taos had him by the arms. Dixon fought them, but it became impossible when Louis and Kalon helped them. They brought Dixon to his knees in front of me.

I shifted back but I didn't face him. Instead, I reached for the black box under the table.

"No, don't!" he yelled.

I picked up the wooden box—it was heavier than it looked—and put it on the table. I opened the lid and a wave of relief coursed through me. The crystals. I picked one up and instantly felt its magic tickling my skin.

We had done it!

I put the crystal back inside the box and turned to Dixon. "What were you doing with them?" Dixon growled but didn't answer. I walked to him and punched him in the gut. Dixon folded in half, groaning. "You're dead either way. Tell me, don't tell me, it'll make no difference."

I shifted my right arm and raised it, poised to strike.

"Wait!" he called out. I paused. "I-I ... Conri told me to run with them. So I did. But you killed him, and I had no use for the damn crystals. I was trying to sell in the supernatural black market."

What if he had sold it before we got to him? The buyer could be someone even worse than Conri. And we might never find the buyer. We were lucky we had found him when we did.

"Any last words?"

Dixon pressed his lips tight.

I lashed my claw across his neck, opening deep gashes. The vampires let him go and he fell at my feet, a pool of blood spreading fast.

I picked up the box with the crystals, glancing at my friends. "Let's go home."

9

RAIKA

Shane had kept his promise. Well, sort of. He hadn't texted me every two minutes, but he did keep me informed about what was going on.

I felt like he was off on this big adventure, while I stayed back watching the babies. I knew my job was important, but I wanted so much more.

The day went by fast, especially since the alpha and one of his betas were away. Vallin stayed in charge, and he wasn't as kind, charismatic, or good-to-look-at as Shane. Between Minsi and Tyren, the library, and the school, I was too busy to notice the time passing.

In the middle of the afternoon, I got a text from Shane.

We've got it. On our way back. Should be there late tonight.

My heart soared. By the moon, they had done it. They had the crystals. All would be well now!

The news that Shane had retrieved the crystals spread fast, and I bet that if we did some research now, his approval rate had gone up tenfold. There was a buzz around town and a spring in everyone's steps.

Everyone talked about being there for when they returned, but Shane had informed Vallin (and me) that they decided to stop to rest. After all, this would be the second night they were away and sleepless, and they should be here early in the morning.

Because of that, Vallin told the pack that Shane and the others would arrive sometime tomorrow. No set hour.

But he and I knew better. He didn't know I knew, though, so after Shane texted me at six in the morning to let me know he was almost here, I texted Lucille and Roman. I thought it would look weird if I was the only one standing there with Vallin to receive them.

I also texted Rue and asked her to stay at the house with Minsi and Tyren, but I shouldn't have bothered. Minsi and Tyren were on high alert, waiting for their brother. When I started moving in my bedroom, they got up and ready to go with me. I texted Rue again, to let her know she didn't need to come, and she replied she would be in the main square, waiting for the group.

I made some to-go coffee for me and Tyren—tea for Minsi—each of us grabbed an apple muffin I had made last night before going to bed, and we headed to the main square. I carried a small brown bag with a muffin and to-go cup for Shane, in case he hadn't eaten yet.

Behind the trees in the distance, the sky was shifting from dark blue to orange as the sun rose. On the way, I couldn't help but notice how much chillier the morning was, even from yesterday. I tightened my thin leather jacket around my body, glad I had brought Minsi's jacket with me and that Tyren had a hoodie on.

The flowers that had been planted a few days ago looked droopy and sad. I made a mental note to check on them. Maybe they needed water. Or was it too cold for them?

Not having the barrier was really messing with everything.

As I expected, there were only a few of us in the main square, standing like silly ducks—Vallin, Roman, Lucille, Rue, Tyren, Minsi, and I. Somehow, Serge had heard and was here too, with two of his friends.

I stood as far from him as I could.

Minsi, Tyren, and I had finished our coffee when the black SUV and the silver sedan rolled in the main square. It was rare to see cars around. They were usually kept away from the town's center, but this time, I knew they were eager to do this.

The cars stopped along the main square and they spilled out—Killian, Lavinia, Taos, Louis, Kalon, Dom, and Shane. My heart squeezed at the sight of him. I let out a huge, relieved breath. He was all right. He seemed all right.

His eyes met mine as soon as he hopped out of the car, then he glanced at his siblings, smiled, waved—Minsi waved back—and he walked to the back of the SUV. The trunk opened and he picked up a medium-sized black box.

Shane walked to one of the corners of the main square, and we all got a little closer. The stone bench and its debris were gone, but the trap door was locked. He placed his hand on the five ridges on the top of the trap doors. A quick sting pricked his fingers.

A hiss sounded as the trap door opened.

I kind of expected some theatrics as he picked up one of the crystals in his hand—by the moon, it really was the crystal!—reached inside the hole, and put it inside. But this wasn't a show, or something entertaining.

It was urgent.

From where we stood, we couldn't see the crystal inside the hole, but Shane was satisfied with it enough to close the hatch, pick up the box, and move to the next corner.

He repeated the process, but this time, when he closed the hatch, a loud hum came from the holes. It spread through the ground, shaking it.

"What's that?" Lucille asked.

"The magic." Lavinia frowned. "But it feels strange."

I held on to Minsi as we all watched the ground.

"This is the crystals activating again, right?" I asked.

"I don't know," Shane said. "This was never done before. We don't know what is supposed to happen and what isn't."

The tremors increased. We crouched down and watched in horror as the buildings around us shook too. The open windows rattled and a couple broke, the unlocked doors opened and closed again with loud booms.

The sound of lightning reached my ears.

But it wasn't lightning.

"Watch out!" Shane yelled. He grabbed my arm and pulled me, Minsi, and Tyren back as the main square's cement pavement cracked open. Gasping or screaming, everyone ran from the square. Serge and his friends fled back to their houses.

Then it stopped.

"Are you all right?" Shane glanced at me, his eyes full of worry. I nodded. He looked at Minsi and Tyren. "You too?" Arms around my waist, Minsi nodded.

"I am fine," Tyren answered.

We all looked around, at each other, at the buildings. Besides some broken windows and unhinged doors, everything seemed all right.

Everything except the wide fault line in the middle of the square.

"That was an earthquake?" Roman asked.

"I don't know," Lucille muttered.

Curious, Shane and some others approached the crack in the pavement. I wanted to go, but didn't want to take Minsi with me.

As if sensing my thoughts, Rue took Minsi and the brown bag from me. "Go," she said.

I offered her a grateful smile and approached the group. Tyren didn't stay behind. We squeezed between Lavinia and Taos, across the gap from Shane and Lucille, who was already way too close to him.

I spied inside.

A thick concrete layer, then just earth. The width became narrower as the gap went on, but we couldn't see the bottom, if there was one.

"What the hell was that?" Killian asked from beside Shane.

"Shh," Lavinia said. She closed her eyes and lifted her hands, fingers splayed in the air, palms toward the gap. "I feel something."

I stared at her. "What do you mean?"

A waft blew up, a faint cloud of red smoke. We all scooted a few steps back. Tyren grabbed my arm, if to pull me back or to feel more secure, I wasn't sure.

"It's magic," Lavinia said, her eyes still closed. "Powerful magic. Ancient magic." Her eyes shot open. "Something is sleeping down there."

"What?" Shane shifted his shocked gaze from her back to the gap. "What do you mean something?"

"I don't know." She lowered her hands. "A creature of sorts? But it doesn't feel like a good thing."

"Your father never told you about something sleeping underneath the town?" Killian asked.

Shane shook his head. "I think I would remember if he had."

"Can't you use your magic to find out?" Lucille asked Lavinia.

Lavinia shook her head. "Whatever it is, it doesn't want to be found."

I frowned. Shane put the crystals back and instead of having the barrier come up again, a crack appeared in the middle of the main square, and apparently a creature was sleeping deep in the earth.

Just a regular day in the Nightshade pack. Because why would anything go smoothly?

"What do we do now?" Roman asked.

Shane sighed. "Right now, everyone should go on about their days. Forget the crack. I'll figure out what's going on."

Roman seemed ready to argue, but nodded. He was the first to walk away.

Lucille looked at Shane. "Why don't you take a break? I can make breakfast for you."

I felt an urge to jump over the crack and push her away from Shane. Instead, I walked away too. After all, I was still the omega and shouldn't be seen hanging around the alpha while he made important decisions.

Shane dismissed her, but I didn't stick around to see or hear if she pushed it. I joined Rue and Minsi at the edge of the square.

"Is everything okay?" Rue asked, her gaze on the group behind me.

"I don't know," I told her. There was no reason to lie to her. "But Shane told us to do our normal stuff while he works on this. That means we move our asses and begin our day."

I took the brown bag from Rue, not sure when I would be able to give it to Shane, if it at all. I steered Minsi toward the library, and Rue left, saying she would be back soon.

Inside the library, Minsi skipped to the rug in the center, where she settled with a book. With a sigh, I went to the front desk and started looking over my giant to-do list. But the words didn't register. I was dying to spy out the window or call Shane. Besides wanting to know what he would do about the crystals and the crack, I wanted to see him. To touch him, to hug him. I hadn't seen him in a little over thirty-six hours and that felt like an eternity.

He had texted me all the time, and last night we had even talked on the phone after his siblings went to bed. He had told me where and how they had found Dixon, about the fight, and finding the crystals in a box.

I gave in to my curiosity and headed to the nearest window.

I took two steps and the front door opened. Shane marched in. I froze, watching as he walked toward me, his brows knotted, his body radiating tension.

He crashed into me, wound his arms around my waist, and pressed his lips to mine. Instantly, I forgot where we were and that someone could walk in on us. I melted into him and kissed him back.

Someone cleared his throat.

I jumped back, but Shane kept his arm locked around my waist, not letting me get too far.

I stared at Tyren.

"It's okay," Shane said. "He knows."

I blinked. "You do?"

Tyren showed me a knowing smile. "I do."

"And you're okay with it?"

He shrugged. "You're too much for him, but yeah, I'm okay with it."

My jaw loosened. "Did I hear you right?"

Shane chuckled. "See? Even he thinks I don't deserve you."

I punched his shoulder. "Don't be stupid." My brows knotted. "But ... what are you doing here? Where are the others?"

"Besides saying hi to my mate, we came to research."

"Yippie," Tyren deadpanned. He walked past us and disappeared between two tall shelves.

"As for the others," he continued, "I sent Lucille to work. Lavinia is still at the crack, trying to find out more about the magic it's emanating. Dom and Vallin went to do the morning rounds along the border since I have my hands and head full, and Killian and the other vampires went back to their posts guarding the pack lands."

"Wait ... you said research?" I asked Shane. "About the crystals? Or the creature?"

"Both," he said.

"But I know most of these books." Aside from some older town records, though, we knew they didn't date back from the pack's foundation. "I don't think there's anything about those."

"I know, but I can't think of anything else." He finally dropped his arm from around me and ran a hand through his hair. "I hoped that once I put the crystals back in, their magic would kick in, and the barrier would come back. Aren't those things linked?" He glanced at the shelves behind us. "Maybe somewhere here I can find how to make the crystals work."

"You think you need to do some kind of spell?"

He shrugged. "I had to do something to open their trap door. Maybe this is no different."

I nodded, but my brows were still knotted. "I can see that, but again, unless we mysteriously find something in the pack's older records, I'm sure there's nothing about the crystals here."

Shane leaned against the front desk's tall counter and crossed his arms. "I don't know what else to do. The crystals are back, but don't seem to be working. I can't make the barrier appear again, and now there's a creature sleeping under our feet."

I turned to him, ran my hands over his toned arms. "You'll figure it out. And I'm here to help you with anything." He leaned into me and his lips brushed mine. "Wait. I have something for you." I reached to the other side of the counter and grabbed the brown bag. "I thought you might not have had any breakfast yet."

His lips curled up and he took the bag from me. "You brought this for me?"

"Well, if I hadn't, would you have had breakfast with Lucille?" That damn invitation earlier still stung.

Shane chuckled. "Still jealous?" He wrapped his big arms around my waist. "You don't need to be, Raika. There's no one else for me." He pressed his mouth to mine and I parted my lips to him, but then Shane stilled. "We have company."

Two seconds later, I heard them. Damn Shane and his alpha hearing. He probably knew who it was, but I didn't, so I disentangled myself from him and took a large step back.

The library's front door opened and Killian and Lavinia

walked in. I relaxed, and when Shane reached for my hand, I let him have it.

"What is it?" Shane asked, all businesslike.

"Dom and Vallin are still out, but so far, no sightings," Killian reported. "No Whitecrest wolves, and no sign of the barrier."

"You thought the barrier could appear slowly?" I asked.

Lavinia nodded. "It was my idea. When it came down before, it didn't just blink away. It slowly opened up, as if it was water going down the drain. I thought that maybe the crystals had reactivated the barrier and it was slowly reforming."

"But it isn't," Killian said.

"Shit." Shane exhaled.

"I was trying to figure out the magic and what is deep in the gap when I had an idea," Lavinia said. "You told us your father didn't mention anything about the creature, but what if you could ask him?"

Shane shook his head once. "What do you mean?"

"To be honest, I'm spitballing here, but maybe we could ask Almae to come back. She's powerful and with her help, I might be able to tap into the underworld and find your father and—" She stopped, her eyes wide. "Wait, I have a better idea. What if you go to the underworld?"

"What?" Shane asked.

"I've met one of the princesses of the underworld, demon hunter Erin Belmont. King Tanner is her brother. I could ask her to contact the king and ask if you could go there, if he could facilitate a meeting between you and your father."

Shane's eyes widened. "Is that possible?"

"I don't know, but there's only one way to find out." She

picked up her phone. "If it is, do you want to go? Should I arrange a meeting?"

Shane looked at me, his eyes still big. I could feel the tension radiating from his body. Meet with his father again, even if for a while. That was probably a shocking proposition.

He gulped. "Yes. Do that."

Lavinia turned her back to us as she called the demon hunter, Killian hovering over her.

Once more, I ran my hand down Shane's arms. "Are you okay?"

He let out a long breath. "I don't know. Talk to my father again? I mean, I want to. He's my father. His death was sudden and brutal. But at the same time ... it feels rushed. As if I'm not ready for it."

"You sure are ready for anything," I assured him. "This might not work out, though. Lavinia had this idea, but we don't know if it's feasible. Don't despair before the fact."

"I know." He grabbed my hands in his. "But despite my apprehension, I think this would be a good thing. I have a long list of things to ask him, starting with the crystals and how to activate the barrier."

"And the creature."

"That too. If he knows about it."

"I hope he does." Otherwise, we were doomed. If the previous alpha didn't know, who would?

"Me too." Shane reached for the to-go coffee cup inside the brown bag and took a sip. He made a face.

"It's not hot anymore?"

He shook his head. "Nope."

I took the cup from him. "There's a microwave in the back." And ceramic mugs. "I'll heat it up for you."

I turned and almost ran into Lavinia as she faced us again.

"I talked to Erin," she said. "She confirmed Tanner can call on anyone in the underworld. She'll arrange a meeting for tomorrow if you want."

I gaped at her. "That was fast."

"Fast, but necessary." Shane nodded. "Tell her I want it." He glanced at me. "And this time, I want you to come with me."

I almost asked why, but it didn't matter. My mate wanted me by his side while he met his dead father—a difficult situation for anyone, even for those with great relationships with their parents.

"Sure," I told him.

10

SHANE

I WAS GOING TO MEET MY FATHER.

That kept repeating in the back of my mind as I went on with my day. It was hard focusing on my usual activities—surveying the border, training the soldiers, fixing the town—when there was a huge crack in the pavement right in the middle of the pack lands, and soon I would see my father.

As the townspeople woke up and went about their day, rumors spread. I swiftly cut them back and assured everyone the problem with the crystals would be solved soon. As per my request, only a few knew where I would be going tomorrow—and most of those didn't even know Raika was coming with me.

Of course, everyone was curious about the crack and the creature inside—I couldn't cull that rumor fast enough. Again, I assured everyone that we didn't know what was down there, if there was anything at all. We all felt an earthquake and that might be the sole cause for the crack.

Even though earthquakes were rare around here.

In the evening, I talked to Dom, Vallin, and Killian about

my absence and their duties. They knew what to do, but I couldn't help it.

Before I retreated to my house, Killian asked if I was sure I didn't want him and Lavinia to come with us.

"I would feel better knowing you're here, caring for my people," I told him. It was the truth.

But I also couldn't wait to spend time alone with Raika, even if it was inside the car while we drove to the nearest underworld entrance.

At my house, I baked the lasagna Raika had left in the fridge for us, and Tyren, Minsi, and I ate as a family, even if we barely talked. Tyren wasn't the talkative type, and Minsi had barely spoken a word since I'd come back.

I wished Raika was here. She would have known what to do. I had texted her, invited her for dinner, but she was busy at the library, cataloging materials that had arrived that afternoon. She wanted to make sure everything was set before leaving for two days.

Early the next morning, I woke up, took a shower, ate breakfast, and opened the door for Rue when she came.

"Thanks for doing this," I told her as she walked in.

"Don't mention it." She patted my arm. "I like staying with them."

I knew they liked staying with her too, and that put me at ease.

When Tyren and Minsi came downstairs, I said goodbye to them, picked up my bag, and went to the garage on the side of the house, where my father's pickup truck was. I threw my bag in the backseat and opened the driver's door as Raika appeared at the garage's entrance.

"I heard there's a place for me in that truck," she said with a small smile.

Holy moon, she was so pretty. Today she wore black leather leggings, a black corset top, and high-heeled boots. Her long, wavy hair was loose behind her back, as usual, and her blue eyes shone bright. Her lips were pinker than usual and an urge to erase her lipstick hit me hard.

"It depends." I stalked to her. "What do I get with that?" She raised one eyebrow. Moon, I couldn't resist her. I grabbed her waist, pulled her against me, pressed her against the truck's side, and kissed her.

The bag she had been holding fell to the ground, and she wrapped her hands around my upper arms.

I ravaged her mouth before dragging my lips down her neck. She gasped when I bit down on her skin. "If you plan on leaving this garage today, I suggest you stop this," she said, breathless. "Besides, isn't everyone in the house? They probably can hear us."

I growled but pulled back slightly. "I want everyone to hear us." I leaned into her and whispered in her ear, "I want them to know you're mine. Just mine."

She sucked in a sharp breath.

By the moon ...

I took a large step back before I ripped off her clothes and had her right there. As much as I would love to do nothing else but sleep with her, we had plenty of urgent matters.

With a sigh, I picked up her bag and threw it beside mine.

Raika rounded the truck and hopped in the passenger seat. I sat behind the wheel, turned the engine on, put on my seat belt, and glanced at her.

"Ready?"

She extended her hand to me. I took it. "Now I am."

Smiling, I drove us out of the garage, out of the pack lands, toward the underworld.

THE NEAREST UNDERWORLD entrance was nine hours away, near Winnipeg. I had talked to Tanner on the phone yesterday afternoon, after he confirmed our meeting with Erin, and he told me what to expect.

Raika and I had to stop for gas and lunch once, but other than that, we drove nonstop.

As instructed, I drove out of town and onto a private road leading to a farmhouse. From the outside, the farm seemed to be functional and cared for, but once we crossed the second metal gate before the farmhouse, the glamour fell.

We stood in an empty field with no houses, no crops. Just a large stone wall the size of a three-story building and several warriors dressed in black leather uniforms.

I stopped the truck and glanced at Raika. She offered me a soft smile before climbing out. I picked up our bags and followed her. A blonde woman approached us.

"Norah, hi," I said. I had met the demon hunter briefly before.

"Shane." She dipped her chin at me then looked at Raika. "And you must be Raika. Hi, I'm Norah."

"Nice to meet you," Raika said.

"You too," Norah said. "I'm a demon hunter and work closely with Erin and King Tanner. I'm here to escort you to his palace. Are you two ready?"

I nodded again.

Norah turned to the stone wall.

Two other demon hunters stood on each side of the wall. They touched the walls at the same time and a green line appeared from their hands. It swirled over the stone, until it met in the center and grew, becoming one large green mesh shining bright.

"Through here." Norah gestured for us to follow. She stepped right through the green light.

I held Raika's hand and we walked into the portal.

The world spun for a second, then settled.

I held my breath as I took in the black path in front of us, the hot red lava lake around it, its heat uncomfortable and menacing, the dark gray sky, and the black palace at the end of the path. It was a huge thing that sprawled over the dark landscape, with several turrets that disappeared among the gray. Lightning cut across the darkness, creating creepy shadows everywhere.

"I know it looks terrifying," Norah said as she started following the path. "It's the way the previous king made it, and nothing we've done let us change it."

"Very underworld like, I guess," Raika said.

Norah chuckled. "You could say that again."

More demon hunters were positioned at the palace's entrance and around it.

I frowned. "Why all the security? Isn't it safe here?"

"If you consider that this place once belonged to someone else, and my friends took it from him, then no, it really isn't." Norah stopped by the huge black doors. "Once Tanner, Erin, and their sisters took over the underworld, demons ran from here, afraid they would be killed. They are now all over the human world, causing a lot more chaos than before. But we know what they want is to come back here. To take the underworld back. So we try to be ready for when they do."

I nodded, remembering when that happened about two years ago. My father had mentioned the previous king had fallen to his children, and now the underworld was under new management—a new king and his princess-sisters who vowed to be just and fair.

But good doesn't exist without evil. The balance of things had shifted and that would bring big impact on everything. And at some point, the balance would either be restored, or it would shift to the other side.

That was how things worked.

The doors opened without Norah touching them. Inside, the foyer was as large as a ballroom and as dark as the outside. Black stones, dark gray walls, dark crystal chandeliers, dark framed mirrors on the walls.

We crossed under an archway into a wide hallway. At the end, another set of double black doors greeted us. Once more, the doors opened by themselves, and behind them a female smiled at us.

"Good afternoon," she said. "I'm Lily, King Tanner's assistant." The king of the underworld had an assistant. All right then. "Please, come this way." She gestured for us to continue into the room.

We went in with Lily and Norah flanking us.

At the end of the room, an oversized chair made of black marble stood—the throne—and seated on it was King Tanner. He stood as we approached and I could see he was almost as tall and wide as I was. He looked like a warrior, though he seemed young to be a damn king, especially of the entire underworld. He had short, black curls, and his skin was a smooth light-olive tone. He wore black slacks and a white button-up shirt. Classy, but not overly so.

Beside him was a woman with long red hair, an hourglass figure in a tight black dress, bright red lips, and hazel eyes. She looked a little older than the king.

"Shane, Raika." Tanner smiled at us. "Welcome to my humble home."

"Humble." The female scoffed. "This place is a lot of things: Dark, creepy, gloomy, but certainly not humble."

Tanner rolled his eyes. "Don't mind Princess Jasmin. I don't."

She slapped his shoulder. "I told you to treat me better or I'll walk, you fool. Want to be alone in this damn palace?"

Tanner groaned. "Can we continue arguing later? We have company." Jasmin huffed, crossed her arms, and sat on the throne's arm as if it was a simple stool put there for her. Tanner turned to us. "Sorry about that. I hope your drive here was all right?"

I nodded. "It was, your highness."

The king scoffed. "No. No *your highness* in here. Just Tanner."

The king of the underworld wanted to be called by his first name. Who was I to deny him that?

"I heard you need to talk to a dead person," he said.

"Yeah. My father."

"Oh. Were you tight with your old man?"

I frowned. "Not as much as people think."

"Nevertheless, sorry about your loss," he said and I nodded.

Jasmin looked at her nails. "Are you tired? Hungry? Thirsty? We could have dinner before—"

"No," I said, cutting off the princess, though I hadn't meant to. "The faster we do this, the better." I rolled my shoulders. "Please, take me to see my father."

11

———

SHANE

"Of course." Tanner nodded. "If you're ready, I can take you to the part of the underworld where the souls of the deceased are. We'll be able to summon him from there."

"I'm ready," I said.

He gestured to an archway to the side. "This way."

Although, as Raika and I followed Tanner and Jasmin through the hallway, with Lily and Norah behind us, I didn't think I was ready. My gut clenched and I felt a mix of hatred and longing. My father had certainly not been the worst, but he had been far from being good.

As if sensing my anxiety, Raika squeezed her hand in mine. I glanced at her and she offered me an encouraging smile.

This hallway was short, but still tall and wide, and there was only one set of sliding double doors in here: an elevator. Tanner pressed the button on the dark wall and the doors slid to the side. We stepped into the large, mirror-lined elevator.

There were a handful of buttons on the panel beside

the doors, with symbols I didn't recognize. Tanner pressed the button right in the middle and the elevator started moving.

"This will take a while." He leaned against the mirror and crossed his arms. "So, you're the Nightshade alpha?"

I nodded. "Yes."

"And you're his mate?" Jasmin asked Raika, though it wasn't a question.

"Yes," Raika answered.

"You two form a beautiful pair." Jasmin sized me up and licked her lips. "Really beautiful."

Tanner nudged her with his elbow. "Stop it, Jas. They are mated." She groaned. "Excuse her. It's hard for her to control herself near handsome males. She's half-demon, half-siren, you see." Tanner sniffed the air and narrowed his eyes at Raika. "But what are you?"

Raika frowned. "What do you mean?"

"Sorry, I can't help it. New, improved powers from the underworld," he explained. "I can get a hint of a different scent within you. I can also sense some dormant magic inside you."

Raika paled.

I didn't like what Tanner was saying. Was he joking or something? "What are you talking about?"

Tanner watched Raika and me for four tense seconds. "Nothing. Forget I said anything."

The elevator stopped, a sound dinged, and the doors opened.

Tanner's nonsense was forgotten the moment we stepped out of the elevator and entered a dark room, like everything else in this palace, but this one wasn't a room per se. After fifty yards, the ceiling and the floor ended in a cliff, revealing an infinite landscape of dark mountains cut by streams of red lava and constant lightning.

One lightning zipped down a few feet from the edge of the room, shaking the floor. A second later, thunder echoed through the room, piercing my ears.

I let go of Raika's hand and walked toward the cliff. "What is this place?"

"Impressive, right?" Tanner asked, his tone amused. He was enjoying this. "That is the entrance to the soul vault. Well, that's what I call it. Beyond this, there are gates, leading to where all the deceased are, and it's divided in groups—the evil ones, the bland ones, the good ones, etc. It goes on forever. Anyway, here—" He gestured to his feet, and only then I noticed there were markings on the dark floor. "—is where the magic happens."

Raika stepped back and took a good look at the markings. "It's like a witch's circle."

I spun, taking in the slightly raised marble pieces forming a wide circle right at the edge of the cliff. Four equidistant points around the circle had waist-high marble pillars.

Tanner walked to the nearest one. "Something like that. Though we don't need a witch for this." He placed a hand on top of the black pillar. His palm shone green, and when he pulled his hand away, dark green flames flickered atop the pillar. He walked to the next one. "Just me."

"If you don't want to end up in the soul vault, you better get out of there before he lights them all," Jasmin said to me.

I stepped out of the circle and stood beside Raika. "What happens now?"

"Now, I finish these." Tanner lit the third pillar. "And then we summon your father. But there are some rules." He stood in front of the fourth pillar. "Don't walk in the circle, or like my sister said, you'll end up stuck with him. He won't be able to leave the circle, so don't try to take him out. Even if you could take him out of there, he'll still be dead." Green flames topped the fourth pillar.

I frowned. I hadn't even thought about trying to take my father out of the underworld. "What else?"

Hands behind his back, Tanner strolled back to stand beside us. "He can't stay here forever. You'll have fifteen minutes, then he'll leave and go back to the vault. So, whatever you have to ask, do it fast. Understood?"

I nodded and inhaled deeply. This was it. I was seeing my father again after he was killed right in front of me over a year ago. I wasn't sure how to feel about this.

Tanner spun his hands around each other.

A dark swirl rose from the floor like a small tornado of shadows. It grew taller, a little taller than me. The shadows faded away as if blown by a gust of wind.

And there he stood.

My father.

My stomach knotted.

"We'll give you some privacy," Tanner whispered. "After he disappears, take the elevator to the top floor. We'll be waiting for you."

He retreated, but I didn't spare him one ounce of my attention.

My father looked around, confused. "What is this?" His rough voice was the same. His eyes settled on me and they widened in surprise. "Shane? What is going on?"

"Dad," I whispered, a sudden lump in my throat. This man hadn't been the perfect man, he hadn't been the best alpha, but he was still my father. "Do you know where you are?"

He shook his head. "I ... I know I'm dead. I was in the underworld."

"You're still in the underworld."

"Then, you're dead?" A growl accompanied his words as if the idea of me dying upset him. "No, no. Only your mother is here. You, Tyren, and Minsi are fine. You can't die."

"I'm not dead."

"Then you defeated that demon-wolf? You saved our pack?"

I winced. "Not exactly ..."

My father's head snapped to the side and he finally took in Raika standing by my side. He snarled. "What the fuck is she doing here?"

Raika took a step back, but I reached for her and held her hand firmly in mine. "Dad, Raika is my mate."

His jaw slackened. "W-what? But she's the omega!"

"Because you demoted her family," I snapped. He wasn't going to talk about my mate like that. "We're not here to talk about our relationship. We have other important matters to discuss."

My father crossed his arms and lifted his chin. "You said you didn't defeat the demon-wolf. Your visit is related to that?"

"Sort of." I rehashed what had happened, a short one-minute version, since we didn't have time to waste. "We recovered the two stolen crystals, I put them back, but the barrier didn't come back up. Instead, something like an earthquake went through the pack lands and a crack formed in the square's pavement." My father's jaw tightened more and more with each of my words. "A witch told us there's something sleeping deep below the gap. Tell me you know about it. Tell me how to fix this."

"Fuck," he muttered. "I should have told you everything a long time ago."

"Everything?" I tensed. "Tell me now."

He let out a long breath. "We always told the pack only half of the truth. Our first alpha was good friends with a witch coven, and they enchanted the pack lands, created the barrier, and gave him the crystals to keep the barrier up. But that wasn't all. What do you know about dragons?"

I gaped at him. "Are you saying there's a dragon below the pack lands?"

"Answer the question."

"I ..." My mind went blank because all I could think was ... holy shit, there was a damn dragon sleeping beneath our feet!

"Dragons are the most powerful supernaturals that ever walked the earth," Raika said, filling in for me. My father glanced at her, annoyance written all over his face, but at least he didn't interrupt her. "It's said they actually came from another realm and got stuck here. Because they were so powerful, they were hunted by other supernaturals. Witches, vampires, wolf shifters, demons ... you name it. Everyone wanted their magic. Everyone thought they could harness the dragons' magic and become more powerful. Slowly, the dragons were captured and killed. They became extinct."

My father nodded. "About eight hundred years ago, one of the last dragons was seen flying over Canada. A big hunt started. During a fight, the dragon became injured. It was dying. Ulfang, our first alpha, found the dragon. The witches put the dragon to sleep and they imprisoned the dragon underneath our lands." He paused. "The crystals have two purposes: to keep the dragon asleep and to absorb his magic.

The dragon's magic feeds the already powerful crystals, and with that, the barrier was unbreakable."

I shook my head. "You're saying our ancestors buried a dragon alive and used his magic for their own purpose?" That was beyond evil. "And you went along with it?"

"I came into all of this almost eight hundred years after they did that! There was a long line of tradition and responsibilities I had to follow. Tell me, how are the pack lands now without the barrier? Is it getting colder? The plants seem off? Are you going to bed worried about intruders and sudden attacks? It's because the barrier and the magic inside it became a crutch. I wasn't going to be the one responsible for changing our entire way of life to save a dragon who was dying anyway."

I couldn't believe I was hearing this. "So you imprisoned an innocent dragon because you couldn't be bothered? That isn't right!"

"Innocent? Dragons were predators, like a lion or a bear. Go near them and they would rip you to pieces. If we didn't kill them, they would kill us."

I shifted my weight. It didn't matter. I wouldn't cage a lion if I ever saw one. Well, maybe I would, but just so it wouldn't hurt me until I could return it to wherever it belonged.

"That isn't right," I repeated, my voice lower.

"If that doesn't convince you then what about this," my father started. He walked to the edge of the circle, close to me. "About twenty years ago, the crystals and their power, the power they drew from the dragon, were used for something else."

I crossed my arms. "What?"

His hard gaze shifted to Raika. "Tell me, how is your magic now that the crystals have been disrupted?"

Raika gasped and took a large step back.

My brows slammed down. First Tanner, now my father. "What the hell are you talking about?"

"Let me tell you another story." A small, sly grin took over my father's face. "I know your mother told you why I demoted Kali's family, and I'm guessing that by now you must have told her." He jutted his chin toward Raika. The intonation in the word her sounded as if he was talking about deadly bacteria. "I admit, I was stupid and naive, and I demoted your family to omega because Kali didn't return my feelings. I should have undone it. Several times, I thought about it, especially after I met Petra. But Kali kept asking for some freedom, so I allowed her to go out of town every once in a while. It was the least I could do. However, I didn't trust her so I sent Kortan to follow her a few times. And each time, he reported Kali met the same man. But he wasn't a man, he was a demon."

Raika took another step back.

I shook my head. "Where are you going with this?"

"Just listen," my father snapped. "At first, Kali didn't know who he was. She thought he was human. Then after a few months, Kali got pregnant. No one else in the pack knew who the father was. But I knew it was the demon." I sucked in a sharp breath. "When she told the demon about her pregnancy, he tried to have her killed. So, she hid behind the barrier and never went out again."

"That was why you didn't allow us to leave," Raika whispered. "It wasn't because you wanted to punish us. You were protecting us."

I stared from Raika to my father, back to Raika. "You're buying all of this."

Raika shifted her blue eyes to me, her gaze downcast. "Shane, I think ... I think it's true."

It was like being punched in the gut. "What?" But then ... that would make her half-wolf, half-demon.

Just like Conri had been.

12

RAIKA

A LIGHTNING BOLT CUT DOWN THE CLIFF'S FACE, TOO CLOSE FOR comfort. I jumped back. When the thunder followed, I pressed my hands over my ears.

"The barrier and the crystals neutralized your demon side," Franc continued as if he hadn't just dropped a bomb on us. "And, if your father ever tried finding you, he couldn't. At least, he wouldn't be able to cross the barrier to get to you. But now that the crystals were disrupted, I imagine your demon side isn't so quiet anymore."

I stared at my hands. It was better than looking at Shane and seeing the hurt in his eyes. "The first time was when Conri first attacked." There was no reason to lie anymore. "Phell killed my mother, but when he threw his shadows at me, I was able to deflect them. I didn't think much of it at the time. I thought it had been his magic failing."

Shane went still. He seemed to be barely breathing.

"Maybe the situation was so intense, and being among darkfire, you were able to tap into it yourself," Franc said. "Darkfire is what a demon's dark magic is called."

My magic even had a special name.

I lowered my hands and stared at him. "I did it again, during the last attack, when Shane killed Conri. Dixon had stolen the crystals and I ran after him. But Phell stopped me. He tried killing me, and I turned the darkfire against him. I killed him."

That made so much sense now, but it still made me sick to my stomach.

Franc nodded. "I had several problems with your mother, but I had made her a promise that I would keep you both safe inside the barrier. That is gone now."

A realization came to me. I tilted my head. "You hate me. You always treated me like dirt. But it wasn't because I was the omega, was it?" Franc's jaw ticked, just like Shane did when he was upset or enraged. "It was because I'm half-demon."

Franc stared at me. That was confirmation enough.

"You lied to me," Shane whispered.

I flinched. Dear moon, I wasn't ready to face him. I looked down at the ground. "I'm sorry."

He scoffed. "Sorry doesn't really cut it, does it?"

No, it probably didn't. And I knew that no matter what I said, Shane's anger wouldn't dissipate easily.

I glanced at him. "Shane, we can argue about this later. Right now, focus on your father. We only have a couple more minutes with him."

Shane stared at me for a few seconds, his eyes dark and hard. My heart wilted inside my chest. Then he faced his father, his body coiled, ready to explode. "We have the crystals back, but no barrier, and a sleeping dragon. What's your advice?"

"I ... I don't have any," Franc said simply. "If I knew who

the original witch coven was, I would tell you to contact them and ask them to redo the spell. Keep the dragon sleeping, redo the barrier, and contain Raika's magic."

"Could we try that with another witch coven?" I asked.

Franc shrugged. "If they are powerful enough and okay with keeping the dragon down there, it could work."

Shane frowned. "This witch coven, is there any clue about them? Any hidden pack archive, or whatever?"

Franc shook his head. "If there is, my father didn't tell me about it."

"What about Raika's father?" Shane asked. "Do you know who he is?"

My eyes widened.

"I ..." Franc pressed his lips tight. "I guess I could tell you. His na—" His words broke as the swirl of shadow returned from the ground.

Shane's eyes rounded and he took a step toward the circle. "Wait, not yet."

"I don't—" Franc tried talking, but his words were fading along with him. "Take care, son."

The shadows enveloped him.

Shane darted toward the circle. I grabbed his arm and pulled him back. "Shane, no!"

He jerked out of my grip, shaking my hands away, but he didn't advance. I stepped back, shocked by his sharp movements. What was I expecting? He probably hated me now too.

The shadow tornado disappeared.

The flames atop the pillars snuffed out.

Franc was gone.

Shane and I stood still for a moment, staring at the empty spot where Franc had been a second ago.

Shane put his hand on his waist and let out a long breath.

"Shane," I started, my voice low.

"Don't *Shane* me. I ..." He turned to me, his eyes enraged. "What hurts the most isn't the fact that you are half-demon. That's pretty shocking, but right now, what hurts the most is that you lied to me."

"I didn't lie," I said quickly. "Not intentionally. I didn't know—"

"But you just admitted you used your magic before. You knew about your powers."

"At first, I thought it was a fluke! That something else must have happened. Later ... I was afraid of myself. I thought —I hoped—that if I ignored it, it would go away. I didn't want this."

"It doesn't matter. We talked about this. We agreed, no more secrets! But you hid something big from me."

"It wasn't my intention. I didn't know what was going on, and until a few minutes ago, I had no idea about my heritage. What do you think *I'm* feeling after finding out my father is a damn demon?"

Shane shook his head. "You should have told me, whatever it was, even if you had no idea what was going on."

"I didn't want you looking at me like you are now," I yelled, my voice breaking. The pain and distrust in his gaze freaking hurt.

He blinked, averted his gaze. "I'm done here."

Shane turned and walked to the elevator. He pressed the button and the doors opened. Without looking at me, Shane stepped inside. The doors closed.

He left.

And this time, he had left me of his own accord.

I stayed in that room, jumping each time lightning struck, for a few more minutes. I wasn't ready to go upstairs and face Shane, or anyone else.

By the moon, what I had done? I knew I should have told him about this a long time ago, but I felt so scared of my magic, so ashamed ... I was afraid he would too.

And now he did.

At the same time I wished I could take it back, so we could go back to being the awesome couple we were, I knew I couldn't. We shouldn't. It had come out for a reason.

I had to believe Shane and I would make it through this. After all, he was my mate. Fate wouldn't tie me together to a male who hated my guts, would it?

Could fate be this cruel?

Yes. Yes, it could.

Just like it had been all along. By the moon, I didn't know what was more shocking: my father being a demon, or the fact that Franc had known and he had protected my mother and me.

All of this info, along with the dragon bit ... it was too much for anyone.

As much as I wanted to disappear, I couldn't stay here forever.

I took the elevator to the top floor.

The doors opened and Lily faced me with a wide smile. "There you are. Welcome back."

I stepped out of the elevator and started down the corridor with her. "Where's Shane?"

"I took him to your bedroom," she said.

"Our bedroom?"

"It's getting late. King Tanner offered for you both to sleep here tonight before going home. Would you like me to take you there now?"

I frowned. "Not yet. Is there any place I could go for a walk? Like any area of the palace where I can roam around?"

"Of course." Lily gestured for me to follow her.

She took me through the empty throne room—I asked about King Tanner and Princess Jasmin and she told me they had another meeting somewhere else—down the same hallway we had first come through, but she turned a right before the foyer, and into a wider hallway.

Then she stopped. "You can explore this area. There are plenty of rooms here: drawing room, music room, library, etc. And if you keep following the hallway, you'll find a sunroom that opens to a beautiful night garden. Is this enough?"

"It's perfect." Maybe I could bury myself inside the library and never come out.

"If you need anything, just come this way. There will always be someone right here," she said. I wanted to tell her I didn't need anything, but I thought this was like living and visiting a palace, especially the underworld palace. "Have fun."

"Thanks," I muttered as I turned and began walking, my steps slow and unsure.

I checked the doors and soon found the library.

I gasped as I walked in, sure I had stepped into the dark version of *Beauty and the Beast*. The library was huge, the ceiling so high that I could barely see it, the shelves lining the walls just as tall, with endless balconies, winding stairs, and ladders. Leather couches and thick rugs covered the floor.

Incredibly tall windows covered one of the walls, showing off the black and red landscape outside.

Pushing all my sad and terrible feelings aside, I disappeared between two bookshelves.

Libraries were my happy place, and nothing would ruin that for me.

13

SHANE

I PACED THE OPEN SPACE IN FRONT OF THE LARGE BED, MY ANGER giving place to worry.

Where was Raika?

Lily had brought me to this suite—large, dark, and ostentatious, with heavy furniture and a view of the lava lake below—over two hours ago.

One hour ago, Tanner had sent an invitation for dinner, which I politely declined. Even so, a half-demon brought a cart with our dinner.

I picked at the food—delicious medium rare steak with a creamy butter sauce and au gratin potatoes—and waited for Raika.

Where the hell was she?

At first, I was mad at her. Disappointed.

She didn't trust me. What had she thought I would do if she told me she had magic she didn't understand? Leave her? Lock her away?

But as the clock ticked away, my feelings seemed less jumbled, and a little reason made itself known.

I hadn't been straightforward with her about my curse. Looking back, I wasn't sure when I would have told her about my Shadow Wolf, if things had been different, if I had been able to save the pack well before or after the full moon.

Eventually, I would've had to tell her.

But I had been concerned about her reaction. She already mistrusted me. She thought I had abandoned her and the pack. She thought I hated her. I was afraid that if I told her, she would push me away.

I understood now.

I cursed under my breath and stared at the bedroom's double door, willing it to open and for her to enter. She was probably upset with me now too. Maybe she needed time to calm down.

I sat in bed, picked up my phone, which didn't work down here, and waited.

Next thing I knew, I woke up, twisted in an awkward position, my neck hurting. I glanced at my phone. It was freaking four in the morning ... and Raika wasn't here.

I bolted from bed, now truly worried.

Where was she?

I walked in the hallway and the same half-demon who brought dinner last night appeared from the shadows.

"Can I help you, Mr. Shane?" he asked, his voice too bright for the middle of the night.

"My mate, Raika, where is she?"

"In the library, sir."

Of course. "Where is the library?"

"I'll take you there." The half-demon took me through more dark corridors past silver-framed mirrors and creepy decorations. We went down two floors, turned into several other hallways, until he stopped before half-closed doors. "In here."

"Thank you," I said, pushing one of the door panels open.

At first, I didn't see anything, just the impressively large library. If Raika was in here, it could take weeks for me to find her. If she wanted to leave. This place was paradise to her, and since she was probably still mad at me, she might prefer staying here.

But I didn't need to worry. Raika was on one of the large leather couches right in the library's center, slouched over the couch's arm, a heavy leather bound book in her lap.

I picked up the book, put it on another couch, and sat down beside her. I wanted to wake her up, but I also didn't. She looked so peaceful, her luscious hair fanning around her like a black halo, her skin smooth and radiant, and her lips so plump. She was pretty and pure. There was no one better than her. I knew that just as I knew my love for her would endure anything. It would go on forever, even after we parted from this life.

And I had made her feel bad about her heritage when she couldn't even control it. I had been a jerk and I couldn't take that back.

But I could make it up to her.

I glanced around and found a big wicker basket between the couches with blankets. As gently as I could, I adjusted her body so she was lying on the couch and placed the blanket over her.

Then I settled back on the far end of the couch and watched over her while she rested.

"Shane?"

I blinked, realizing I had fallen asleep too. I sat upright, my neck hurting a little more now, and saw Raika staring at me, her expression guarded.

"Hey." I ran a hand through my messy hair. "What time is it?"

"A little past six in the morning," she answered.

I had dozed off for a couple of hours.

I looked at Raika. There was so much I wanted to say, so much I needed to fix. I opened my mouth, but the words got stuck in my throat.

"Good morning!"

I startled and turned. Lily stood on the other side of the couch. She stared at us with a soft smile. "Did you sleep well? I hope the couch was comfortable enough."

I rubbed at the back of neck. "I ..."

"If you're ready, I'm here to escort you back to the gate," Lily said, her tone chipper.

I looked at Raika, but she avoided my gaze and stood to face the demon.

I frowned. "What about our bags?"

Lily didn't move as she said, "Already packed and waiting for you."

What ... they had packed our stuff back in the bag. Not that I had really touched them, nor had Raika, but still, I didn't like how comfortable and invasive this demon was. Or perhaps everyone in the underworld was like that.

I didn't really care.

"Are you ready to go?" I asked Raika.

She nodded, still not looking at me. I sighed. "Yeah, okay, I guess we're ready to go then."

"Splendid! Please follow me." Lily beckoned us toward the exit. We fell into step behind her. "You'll have to excuse King Tanner and Princess Jasmin. They had planned on seeing you out, but the underworld never stops and they had an urgent meeting this morning."

"It's okay," I said.

On the way out, Raika asked to have her bag and stop in a bathroom—she said she wanted to brush her teeth and wash her face before continuing the trip. That wasn't a bad idea, so I did the same.

After, Lily took us to the palace's front door, where Norah was waiting to escort us back to the farm.

She halted before the truck. "I hope you found the answers you were looking for."

"We found some answers, and more questions."

She scoffed. "Isn't it always like that? Well, good luck with whatever you're doing."

"Thanks." I turned to the truck, wanting to open the passenger door for Raika, but she beat me to it.

She muttered goodbye to Norah and hopped in the truck. I exhaled, trying to remain calm, and joined her inside the truck.

I opened my mouth to talk to her, but she promptly rested her head back on the seat and closed her eyes.

This was going to be one long drive.

THE DRIVE BACK WAS TENSE.

Raika settled on the passenger seat, turned on the music loud enough so it was hard to talk over, and turned to the window. She closed her eyes and either slept or pretended to sleep.

Several times, I opened my mouth, not really knowing

what to say, but I wanted to. But when the beat of the music intensified, or when I glanced at Raika and saw her avoiding me, any words I had imagined saying fled my brain.

I gripped the wheel tight, a sliver of anger coming back, but not for the same reason. Couldn't she make this a little bit easier for me?

Three hours into the road, I stopped for gas since the truck drank gas like water. Raika woke up then and went to the bathroom. She came back with two to-go coffee cups and a brown bag.

When I sat beside her again, she offered them to me. "We didn't have breakfast. I thought you might be hungry."

A lump got stuck in my throat. Even disappointed in me, she still thought of me. I got the cup and one of the glazed doughnuts from inside the bag. "Thanks."

I took a sip of the coffee, a bite of the doughnut, put the coffee in the cup holder at the truck's dashboard, and started driving.

As I steered us back into the highway, I glanced at Raika. She still looked out the window, half her body turned away from me, but somehow, I knew ... deep down, I knew this was a small bump in the road. Any relationships had them, even the most perfect ones. It was impossible not to.

And sometimes, all you needed was a little time to digest the problem, for the anger to fade away.

Tonight, I would invite her over for dinner with Tyren and Minsi, and I would apologize properly for my reaction.

Feeling a little better, I stepped on the gas.

We drove for several more hours. Finally, we took the first back road off the highway that led deep into the forest, toward the pack lands.

Suddenly, a great force slammed into the car from the

side. I held on to the wheel, tried controlling the car, but it was impossible. The truck was pushed off the road, into a small hill.

"Raika," I called as the truck flipped.

Everything happened fast, and pain spread through my shoulders and my lower back as the truck rolled a couple of times, and then stopped against a tree, turned upside down.

My mind felt heavy, my body too, as if I was swimming in syrup. I blinked, trying to stay awake, even though the pain was too great.

"Raika," I called again.

"H-here," she whispered, her voice faint.

I turned, my neck hurting, and saw she was like me, hanging from the seat because of the seat belt. The airbags had gone off, the windshield was broken, and the front of the truck was smoking.

A sharp pain came from my shoulder. I reached for it and saw a little blood staining my fingers. Shit.

"Are you okay?" I asked.

"I think so."

"We need to get out." I braced myself with one hand and pressed the button to release the seat belt. I fell down on the truck's top, all twisted, but I squirmed and turned toward Raika. "I'll help you. Use your arms."

She put both arms over her head, pushing against the truck's bent ceiling and I released her seat belt. I tried cushioning her fall, but there wasn't much I could do. Like me, she fell into a heap and yelped. Now that I was closer to her, I could see a trickle of blood on her forehead and her upper arm.

"Come on."

We crawled out of the truck. I stood, my head spun for a

second, my body screamed. Raika stood beside me, but leaned against the truck.

The fog in my vision cleared.

A dozen wolves surrounded us. Wolves with bright white spots on their brown or gray fur.

The Whitecrest pack.

"What the—?" I clenched my fists. "You're the ones who did this?"

No one shifted to talk to me. Instead, they lunged at us.

My rage spiked and I started shifting.

But I didn't shift into my normal wolf.

The Shadow Wolf took over.

14

RAIKA

MY HEAD POUNDED, MY ARM THROBBED, MY LEGS FELT LIKE they were on a rocky boat on a stormy sea, but I shifted.

As soon as I turned into my wolf, the healing sped up, and I felt a little better. Less dizzy, less painful.

A gray wolf with white paws rammed at me, pushing me into the truck's broken door. Smaller, I slipped from under his grip and pawed at his muzzle. I pushed him down on the ground and snarled.

Holy shit ... I was going to have to kill, wouldn't I? It was one thing to kill demons who had kept my pack enslaved for a full year, but other wolves? Neighbor packs?

I hesitated.

Another wolf jumped on my back and the two of them worked together to roll me to the side and pin me down.

I jerked frantically, snapping my teeth or moving my paws to deflect their bites.

Teeth closed around my shoulders.

Then the wolves were gone.

I blinked as Shane appeared in front of me, in his Shadow

Wolf form, and held both wolves up by their hind legs. He threw them and they flew several yards. One hit a tree with a sickening crunch and the other rolled on the dirt, before yelping and darting away.

On two legs, Shane's chest moved fast and he snarled at the wolves.

I glanced around and gasped. There were at least eight bodies at our feet, some still in their wolf forms, others back to their human selves. But all of them bleeding, broken ... probably dead.

The other four were nowhere to be seen. One had run, maybe the other three had too.

Shane turned his red eyes to me and I stilled.

I could see why they would run.

Shane, I whispered through the mind link.

It was useless. When he was in this form, he couldn't hear me.

I retreated, rounding the car until I was with the forest at my back. If the Shadow Wolf took over, if Shane didn't recognize me, I could run. Not that I thought I could get away from him like this, but I would at least try.

Shane moved with me, his teeth bared, his shoulders hunched, as if he was sizing up his prey. He looked like a monster out of a horror movie.

Fear bloomed in my chest, but I pushed it back.

No, no time for that. This was my mate. Our bond was stronger than any damn curse, I had to believe that.

I shifted back and stood there, facing him with my chin held high. "Shane. Come back to me."

A growl ripped through his throat.

He took three fast steps toward me. I flinched, but locked my muscles. I wouldn't move!

Then he stopped. He stared at me, his head tilted.

The first thing to change were his eyes. The red faded away, and his warm brown came back. Then the rest of him shifted.

Naked body shaking, Shane stood a handful of feet from me. "Raika, I'm sorry." He glanced down at his hands, as if he didn't recognize them. "I didn't—"

I ran to him, launched myself at him, and embraced him. With a sigh, Shane wound his arms around my waist and buried his head on my neck.

He inhaled deeply. "I've lost control. The Shadow Wolf is stronger. He took over. I couldn't do anything." He glanced back, to the dead bodies around the truck. "I don't remember any of it."

I frowned. Shit, this wasn't good. We were halfway through a month, still two weeks from the next full moon. But at the same time, I knew that if the Shadow Wolf hadn't taken over, Shane and I might not be alive now. Shane was strong, but the two of us against twelve? Those were bad odds.

I ran my hands over his bare shoulders. "It's okay. You're okay now. We are okay."

He stared at me, his eyes rummaging over my forehead, my forearm, my shoulder. All the wounds were practically healed, thanks to our wolf traits.

He cupped my cheek. "I'm sorry."

"I told you, it's fine."

"No. For yesterday."

My breath caught. "You aren't mad at me anymore?"

"No, I'm not. I wasn't mad at you in any moment. I was just shocked. I'm known to have a hot temper and it gets the best of me." He shook his head. "Raika, I'm sorry. I don't know why that is so hard to say, but it's true. I overreacted, I acted like a jerk, and—"

"I should have told you sooner." That was something I couldn't change now, but I would forever regret.

"Probably, but it has been only two weeks since we defeated Conri, since you discovered you could semi-control darkfire. And we were busy with the pack, searching for the crystals, looking for a Nightmist witch." He paused. "And there was me too. I understand why you held back. It isn't easy to tell someone you care about your darkest secret. You were afraid of my reaction."

"You can't be all right with me being a half-demon," I said. "Damn, I'm not all right with it." Since hearing it from Franc, I felt the urge to pinch myself all the time, to make sure this wasn't a nightmare.

"I ... I can't say I love it, but I love you." He stared into my eyes, his gaze soft. "Whatever happens, wherever this leads us, we'll do this together." My chest constricted and my eyes brimmed with tears. "Hey, I didn't want to make you cry."

"Just shut up and kiss me already," I whispered.

A smile spread over his lips. "You don't need to tell me twice."

He lowered his head to mine, taking my mouth with his. The kiss started slow, but sped up, and desire flooded my veins.

Shane retreated with me. We almost tripped over a broken tree branch, and that was when I remembered where we were and the bodies littering the forest just a few yards from us.

I didn't want to sleep with Shane here, in this situation.

I broke the kiss, breathing hard, and whispered, "We should stop."

He nodded, his forehead brushing against mine. "You're right." With a sigh, Shane stepped back. "We need to get dressed, call the pack, clean up this mess, and figure out what's going on."

He walked back to the truck. My stomach knotted looking at it. By the moon, we had been inside it and now it looked so beat up, it was a wonder we weren't in worse shape.

Shane rescued our bags from the truck and threw mine at me. "We have a lot to do."

That we certainly did.

LESS THAN TWO HOURS LATER, a group showed up to help us. Dom, Vallin, Killian, and Taos. They asked Shane what was going on, but Shane said we would talk about it when we got back in town, and then he would tell them what had happened.

In near silence, they picked up the bodies, covered them in blankets, hauled them into the back of another truck. I felt sick watching. But Shane said he wanted the bodies delivered to the Whitecrest pack. Even if this was the beginning of a war, he would have wanted his body returned, so he was doing the same.

They also hooked up the truck wrapped around the tree to cables in the back of another truck. Together, we flipped it over, and with the cables, had the truck brought to the side of the road. Vallin was already on the phone with the insurance company, probably talking about how to have the car picked up and all that. He would spin a beautiful lie about losing control of the truck, going down the hill, but thankfully not being hurt. If there was any problem with the person coming to collect the truck and take it to a car shop, Killian would intervene with his compulsion. But we all knew the truck had been totaled.

It was past noon when we arrived back at the pack. Lavinia was waiting for us at the town hall, with lunch—bless her—and a potion she said would help with pain, if we still had any.

While we ate the delicious caprese panini, Shane told Dom and Vallin to patrol the pack lands' border. The White-crest pack had deliberately attacked us. He didn't want to be caught by surprise again.

When they walked out, Killian closed the door behind us. Only him, Lavinia, Shane, and I remained inside his office.

He leaned on the closed door and crossed his arms. "So, what happened?"

Seated behind his desk, Shane scoffed. "Do you want to know everything, or the abbreviated version?"

"Tell us everything," Lavinia said. She was seated on one of the chairs across the desk, and I took the other.

Shane and I shared a glance before he told the events of the past two days. He started with arriving at the underworld, the heavy demon hunter presence, how the new king was easygoing, and his sister a little horny.

Then he told them about meeting his father, the crystals, and the dragon.

"A dragon?" Killian asked. "But ... those have been extinct for centuries. So have dragon shifters."

"Yeah, well, maybe they became extinct faster because of what my ancestors did," Shane said, his tone heavy.

"All right, a dragon," Lavinia said. "What do we do about it? What your father suggested? Ask another coven to recreate the spell, or invent a new one, to reactivate the crystals and make a new barrier? Or will you wake up the dragon?"

"I don't know." Shane sighed and ate the last bite of his panini. "If we let the dragon go, the crystals won't work. There will be no barrier. But how can I sleep with a clear conscience knowing we're keeping such an amazing creature buried underneath our feet?"

That was exactly how I felt. Even knowing the right thing to do, it wasn't an easy thing. Freeing the dragon meant dooming the pack lands.

And having my powers out in the open.

"There's more," I said and everyone looked at me. Shane trusted Killian and Lavinia. They had been his allies for a long time now, and I knew he trusted them more than he trusted Dom and Vallin—thus why they weren't here. So, I told them what Franc said about me, my powers, and my heritage.

It might not be the most important detail, but things were going sideways, and having all the cards on the table might make a difference.

Lavinia rested her hand on my arm. "I'm so sorry you had to find out this way."

I nodded. I felt sorry too, but not because I had found out, but because it was the truth. I still hadn't come to terms with it, and I wasn't sure I ever would.

I cleared my throat. "Anyway, then we were attacked by Whitecrest wolves on the way back."

Shane's brows curled down. "I still don't understand that."

"Didn't you say Delco, the Ironfang alpha, had told you the Whitecrest had been talking to Conri?" Killian asked.

Yes, I remembered that.

"But Conri is dead," Shane said. "Whatever alliance they

had, it's gone now. However, it doesn't matter why they did it, this attack can't be ignored. They attacked the alpha directly. They wanted to kill us. Quiet and simple. If that isn't reason to start a war, I don't know what is."

I pushed half of my panini aside. It was delicious but this talk was all doom and gloom, and my appetite had waned. "You won't start a war, though, right? We have too many problems at the moment, and we don't have enough wolves to fight."

"I don't want to start one, no, but I won't stand by and let them play with us." Shane paused, his jaw hard. "I'll call for a meeting of the alphas. I'll show them I might not be my father, but I won't stand for this crap."

"A meeting is a good idea," I said. As long as it didn't turn into a big fight right then. I hoped Shane took his betas, plus Killian and some of his vampires.

"What about here?" Shane asked with a sigh. "Anything that we should know? Any news in the day and a half we were gone?"

Lavinia and Killian exchanged a glance.

Oh, that couldn't be good.

"There is, but you'd better come with us," Killian said.

Shane tensed. "What is it?"

Lavinia stood from the chair. "It's better if you see it with your own eyes,"

15

SHANE

I DIDN'T KNOW WHAT TO EXPECT.

It all felt mysterious while Lavinia and Killian guided us to the back of the town hall, where an off-road Jeep was parked. We hopped in and Killian drove us onto the road exiting the town and the pack lands, toward the north, where there was nothing beyond our lands but more forest and lakes. Right before crossing the border, he veered into the forest.

He drove for another few minutes, then stopped. "Come," he said, getting off the car.

That expression about suspense being a killer was a real thing.

I glanced around as I climbed out of the Jeep, but saw nothing unusual. The hard ground, bushes, trees, vines, rocks … "What is it?"

Killian walked past a tight line of trees. I followed and then halted.

"Almae?" I asked, confused. "What are you doing here?"

The old witch stood from where she was crouched down

and that was when I saw it. Beyond her, the land was black. Not just the land. Everything—the trees, the bushes. It was like a wildfire had cut through here and left ashes behind.

"What is this?" I walked closer. "What is happening?"

Right by my side, Raika gasped. "By the moon."

"I spotted this last night on one of my patrols," Killian said.

Lavinia walked to Almae. "He called me and I came to check it, but it's like nothing I have ever seen. So I called Almae, and to my surprise, she was actually on the way here."

Almae offered us a soft smile. "Surprised to see me?"

"You could say that," I mumbled, my eyes still on the black land.

"She arrived an hour later and I brought her here," Lavinia continued.

"They spent most of the night here," Killian said. "But they came back early this morning."

"And it was worse," Almae said, her voice rough. "The poison has advanced a foot more, taking more of the forest."

"Wait." I shook my head. "Poison?"

Almae nodded. "Lavinia and I were able to join our powers and find the source."

"And?" Raika asked, her tone as shocked as I felt.

"The crystals you've brought back," Lavinia said. "They aren't the same. We think they were depleted of their magic and filled with some kind of magical poison. It's affecting the land. Killing it."

I froze.

Raika's face paled. "Wait. That means ... Dixon wanted us to find the crystals?"

"That explains how it was so easy to find him, to kill him and the demons who were with him, to bring the crystals back." By the moon, I had been such a fool. I should have questioned this instead of celebrating. "But why? He let me kill him so I could bring poisoned crystals back here? To what end?"

Almae shrugged. "That I cannot say. The only thing I can know is that this poison is moving fast. If we don't find a way of neutralizing it, it'll consume the pack lands within two weeks, maybe less."

My jaw hurting from clenching my teeth too tight, I marched back to the Jeep. "Then we take the crystals out."

"We already tried that," Lavinia said.

I halted. "How did you open the trap doors?"

"We asked Tyren to try it," Killian answered. "It turns out the alpha's blood isn't just in the alpha."

I wasn't sure what to feel about Tyren being brought into this. I had promised him I would let him help me more, but it was so damn hard when all I wanted was to keep him safe.

"We tried taking the crystals out with magic," Lavinia said. "And by force. Nothing works."

I hadn't even decided what I would do about the crystals and the dragon, and now another impossible task had piled up on top of the rest. If we couldn't take the crystals out, the land would die, and the dragon would remain deep in the earth. Would the poison kill him too?

I ran a hand through my hair. "There has to be something we can do." I glanced at Raika. "Maybe a book in the library about magical poisons?"

"There are a few, but I haven't read them all," she said. "I'll take a look at them."

"That's a good idea," Almae said. "Meanwhile, Lavinia and I will continue trying anything we can think of. But if Raika doesn't find anything, I suggest we call Thea and other witches. We might need more help to solve this problem."

I considered this. Hadn't my father said we would probably need a powerful witch coven to reactivate the crystals? This wasn't much different.

I nodded once. "Do whatever you have to."

Beside me, Raika tilted her head. "Almae, you said you were on your way here when Lavinia called you. Why is that?"

Almae's lips turned down. "I had a vision."

"A vision?" I asked, confused.

"Almae has the gift of foresight," Lavinia explained.

"Well, it can be a gift or a curse," Almae added. "And it doesn't always work how I want it to. Visions come when they want to, not when I ask. Anyway, I saw a vision of a great evil showing itself here, in the center of the Nightshade pack."

"A great evil?" Raika asked. "What does that mean? Did you see any details?"

Almae shook her head. "The vision wasn't clear. I couldn't see much, but I felt it." She pressed a hand to her chest. "Right here. It'll happen soon."

I frowned. A great evil? "It can only be the dragon. The crystals aren't working. The dragon isn't contained anymore. It'll wake up." Shit, one more problem to add to the list.

"It could be," Almae said, though she didn't know about the dragon yet. "If I see more details, I'll let you know."

I headed back to the Jeep and said, "All of this ... the crystals, the poison, the dragon. It stays between us. Killian, make sure no one comes this way when patrolling. Last thing we need is people finding out about this and panicking."

16

SHANE

That night, I barely slept. I was glad to be home with Minsi and Tyren. I would have felt even better if Raika had come over, but she had retreated to the library to research the poison and hadn't emerged since.

I stopped there before going to sleep and told her I would spend the night with her, but she threatened to un-mate me if I did. At least that brought a smile to my lips.

She promised to go to bed soon too, though I knew she would lie down on the rug and pillows in the center of the library, nap for a short while, and then continue her research. Nothing I said or did would change her mind. I trusted her and let her do her thing.

I had also called an alphas' meeting. I insisted we all meet on neutral ground today. It was urgent and no one could miss. If someone was traveling, they needed to come back ASAP. I didn't want to be accommodating or nice. They were older and more experienced than I was. I couldn't show them an ounce of weakness.

We agreed to meet two hours south of here, away from the pack lands, early in the afternoon. I sent Dom and Vallin there first to prepare the place and to erect a tent big enough for six alphas and their betas, with six chairs in the center.

Killian insisted he come with me. He promised he would stay in the car, far from the meeting, but he would keep his senses open and if he heard anything strange, he would come to help.

I prayed it didn't come to that.

When I arrived at the tent in the middle of the forest, I wasn't the first one there. Besides Dom and Vallin, Delco, Ironfang's alpha, and his betas were here.

We greeted each other.

"I haven't forgotten your help," I told him.

"Oh, yes, you still owe me a favor," Delco said. He sounded pleased with that. "I'll let you know when you can repay it."

I didn't like the sound of that.

Next, the Boldridge alpha and his betas arrived. He barely paid me any attention as he took his chair in the center of the room, and his betas stood behind him.

The alphas of Wildtail and Warhide strolled in like they owned the place. They glared at each other and the tension escalated tenfold. With the war they were fighting against each other, it would be a miracle if they didn't attack each other in here.

Almost half an hour late, the Whitecrest alpha arrived. Dressed in all white, Nortrix didn't even look at me as he stepped under the tent and took his chair. His betas, though, had their hands on the hilt of daggers strapped to their belts.

I held back a scoff. As if wolves fought with weapons.

The large tent felt tight and charged with six alphas and twelve betas.

"So," Delco started once we were all seated. "What is this meeting for?"

I faced each one of them for two seconds, before saying, "Yesterday, I was attacked by Whitecrest wolves." The other wolves seemed surprised, but Nortrix didn't even flinch. "I killed eight of the twelve wolves who attacked me and sent their bodies back to you. I believe you received them?"

Nortrix finally looked at me. "I'm just upset they didn't finish you off as I ordered."

I sucked in a sharp breath. "So you did order It." I wasn't expecting him to admit it. Moreover, I had gotten a full confession in front of the other alphas.

"I punished the other four who came back." Nortrix leaned forward on his chair. "Next time, they won't fail."

I gripped the arms of my chair. "Why do you want to kill me?"

"Wouldn't you like to know?"

He was getting on my nerves. "Is it because of Conri? What did he promise you?"

"Conri." Nortrix laughed as if I had told a joke. "He was an errand boy and he couldn't even get that right."

Wait, what? Conri was an errand boy? What did that mean? "Who was Conri working with? What did he want with my pack?"

"Listen, boy—"

I slapped the chair's arm and it rattled underneath me. "I'm not a *boy*. I might be young, younger than all of you, but I will not be treated like a child. You will respect me and—"

A growl started from my right and in two seconds, the Wildtail and the Warhide alphas were on the floor, mauling at each other. Their betas didn't even try to separate them—they joined the fray.

Oh, shit.

I tried getting to them, prying them apart. Dom, Vallin, Delco, and his betas helped me.

But Nortrix snickered. As I pulled one alpha back and Delco pulled another, I glanced at Nortrix. He walked toward me, put his hand on my shoulder. "We're not done, boy." He grazed his long nails over my upper arm, drawing blood.

I snarled at him and I would have grabbed his neck and demanded an explanation, if I wasn't busy holding another wolf.

He wiped a finger at the scratch and smiled at me. Then he walked out of the tent with his betas.

What the hell?

It took us a few minutes to fully separate the Wildtail and the Warhide packs—they left shortly after, yelling bloody murder at each other—and by then Nortrix was far gone.

This meeting had solved nothing.

Though I had found out the attack yesterday hadn't been a random action or an error. The Whitecrest pack wanted me dead.

Delco placed a hand on my shoulder. "I remember when I became alpha. I was young too and it took me a while to earn the respect of the other alphas."

"Did they try killing you?"

He chuckled. "Not that I can remember, but who knows? Maybe one of the attacks from that time was one of them in disguise."

This was ridiculous. Five strong packs nestled in the same region in northern Canada and we couldn't act like adults and get along?

"Thanks for coming," I told him.

He nodded. "We'll talk soon."

I frowned, not liking that. I watched as he and his betas left, sure he would ask something of me that I wouldn't be willing to do.

17

RAIKA

I LEFT THE SCHOOL AND WALKED ACROSS THE MAIN SQUARE—
avoiding the huge crack in the center—toward the library.
Despite all the heavy things weighing on our shoulders, life
didn't stop and there was a lot of work to do around here.

Last night, I had spent hours reading the books about
poisons that I could find. Some I had already read before, but
I didn't remember them all that well. I napped with a book in
my lap for a couple of hours, but then went right back to
work before sunrise. I still had a few more books to comb
through, but so far I hadn't found anything.

To be honest, I didn't think I would, but I had to hold on
to hope.

Lavinia and Almae had been at the library early in the
morning, asking for some books about enchanted crystals.
They hoped they would find what kind of spell it was used to
poison the crystals, or something similar that could lead
them to a way of rendering the crystals useless. That meant
we would never have the barrier back, but from where I was
standing, that seemed like a faraway dream anyway.

If it wasn't the poison, then it was the dragon. I knew Shane was still torn about it, not because he hadn't made the decision—in his mind, he had already chosen to save the dragon—but because he had to admit he was ready to doom this place.

Our home.

And then we all would have to adapt to extreme cold, build fireplaces or other heating devices in all our houses. We would also have to learn how to live without a barrier. As far as I knew, no other pack had something like that, so I was sure this was the least concerning, though right now, with all the craziness happening around us, I was a little worried about the pack's safety. Without the barrier, anyone could enter, and as proven yesterday, we weren't even safe from the neighboring packs.

A cold breeze blew past me and I groaned. It was June, for crying out loud. Even here, it was supposed to be warm, wasn't it? Honestly, I had no idea. I had been born and raised with the barrier over my head. I didn't know how it was supposed to be. Perhaps even the weather was messed up now because of the poison? That was something we should research.

I reached the library's door and halted as another gust of wind blew past, bringing her scent to my nostrils. I spun around as Lucille walked toward me, a soft smile on her lips.

"Hey there."

"Hey." I frowned. "What's up?"

"I've been thinking. Shane agreed we could train, but apparently, there's a lot going on around here and most of the male wolves are too busy." She cupped her mouth and whispered, "The alpha and his huge to-do list. Who knows what's in that?"

I knew. I helped him make his long to-do list. "Right?" was all I said, feeling pathetic.

"So, since no one tells us what's going on and we're fixing the town and being underutilized, I say we should practice ourselves. You, me, Jena and, Celina. What do you say?"

I opened my mouth ... what would I say to her? She knew about the missing crystals and Shane's curse, but she had no idea about the rest—the dragon, the Whitecrest attack, the poison.

I smiled at her. "I would love that." I really would, but chances were, it wouldn't go as planned. And if they really got together for practice and called me, I would think about it. If I had time, I would join them. If I was busy—when wasn't I busy?—I would make some excuse.

"Great." She tilted her head and her smile widened. "I think that when things are a little smoother here, we could have a girls' night out. Or, actually, a girls' night in. At my house. All the girls around our age, a cheese and salami platter, cheap wine, and a funny movie."

I offered a tight smile, my heart strings tugged hard. "I really would love that." I had never done anything like that and the prospect of having real friends, girl friends, was unreal. If Lavinia was still here, I would rope her in too.

"Great." She took a step back. "I'll go back to my chores, but I'll keep in touch. I'll create a group chat so we can talk about our first practice."

"Sounds good."

Lucille waved, turned, and walked away. I watched as she headed toward the building beside the town hall, where a coffee shop and a restaurant had been before. Those were also under renovations, but I wondered now if that wasn't wasted time. I knew people were eager for normalcy, but there was too much to be done everywhere else.

Lucille swiped her blond hair from over her shoulder, a movement I always connected to bitchiness inside my mind, but now looking at her, I wondered if it wasn't just her way. A habit she had and didn't even notice.

Oh, Lucille could be a bitch, but maybe, maybe she could be more? Practice together, girls' night in? I like the sound of those.

With a sigh, I walked into the library and found Lavinia and Almae still hunkered down over a long table covered in books, researching the crystals.

Lavinia lifted her head from the books. She smiled at me. "You look ... happy?"

I shrugged. "I probably shouldn't, with everything going on."

"Nonsense," Almae said. She glanced at me. "I've lived through many battles and wars, lost many friends ... you need to find the light amid the darkness, otherwise what are you even living for?"

I nodded, thinking about Shane, how he made me feel. About Minsi, and Tyren, and even Lucille and her crazy ideas. Tiny moments that mattered a whole lot.

"True, but while we bask in the light, we need to find a solution for the darkness." I sat down across the table. "How's research going?"

Lavinia groaned. "Not good." She pushed a book in my direction. "But you can help us." She batted her lashes at me.

I chuckled. "I have to take more stuff to the school, but I can squeeze in a book or two before that."

"I'll owe you some coffee," she said. "And some cinnamon rolls."

Almae shook her head. "You and cinnamon."

"What? Cinnamon is life!"

I smiled, watching them for a second. Here with Lavinia and Almae, I wasn't in a girls' night in per se, but we were also having our own moment.

And I would add those up without prejudice.

18

SHANE

AS I ARRIVED BACK IN TOWN WITH DOM AND VALLIN, DARK clouds seemed to follow me in the sky, matching my mood. The late afternoon darkened. It seemed it would rain soon.

It only got worse when I hopped out of the car and saw Raika leaving the library and Roman running to her with a wide smile. I tried not to, I swear I did, but I couldn't help it. I focused on my hearing and watched as he walked to the school with her.

"Can you talk now?" Roman started, his voice sounding awkward.

"Sure," Raika said.

"I was thinking ... I've prepared a Bolognese lasagna this morning, you know, for tonight's dinner, but it's a lot for just one." Holy shit, I didn't know if I was more annoyed he was asking my girl out, or at the stupid way he was doing it. "What do you think of stopping by and having dinner with me?"

"Hm ..." Raika glanced over his shoulder, right at me. "I'm sorry, Roman, but I'll have to pass." She pointed back to the library. "I have a big task I'm working on and I'll probably spend another night between books."

"Then I could bring the lasagna to you and—"

They stepped into the school and I forced myself to stop being a creep. I might not trust Roman, but I trusted Raika.

The sky rumbled, announcing incoming rain, and a cold breeze rushed by. Was rain in June normal for Canada? I had no idea what was normal or not anymore. I might have to learn now that we didn't have a barrier.

If our time here lasted. With the dragon, the poison, the Whitecrests' threat ... I wasn't sure of anything anymore.

I turned to the town hall and Lucille stepped right in my way. "Hi." She tucked a strand of blond hair behind her ear. "I heard you met with the other alphas. Everything okay?"

I nodded. "It will be."

That was probably a lie, but she didn't need to know anything. Not yet, at least.

I stepped into the lobby and Lucille followed. "Is there anything I can help you with? Read some reports? Maybe write some reports? Or—"

I spun around and faced her. I had nothing against Lucille, but I was already in a bad mood, and pushing me like this didn't help.

"Lucille, I've got a headache," I lied. "I really could use some peace and quiet right now."

"Oh." Her shoulders sagged. "It's ... yeah, you should rest. Take something for the pain and rest. I'll see you later, then." She offered me a forced smile, then walked out of the town hall.

Dom walked in after she left. "Well done."

"Don't start," I said with a snarl.

"What? Just because she has been into you since we were

five years old? You kept pulling and pushing her all of our teenage years. If she's still holding on to hope that you will pull again, it's your fault."

I groaned. He was damn right. I really had to talk to her. Maybe even tell her the truth about Raika and me. That way, she would finally understand we would never get back together.

"Just ... shut up," I told him as I headed toward my office. I regretted my words, but I wouldn't take them back now.

Unfazed, Dom followed me into my office. Vallin, with whom I didn't have much of a relationship, stayed outside.

Dom plopped down on one of the chairs across the desk. "You need to relax, boss."

"Don't call me that." I didn't sit on my chair. Instead, I went to the window and looked out at the town. From here, I had a good view of the main square, the school, the infirmary, and the library. A handful of wolves walked up and down, going on about their chores.

"That's what you are now."

I turned my back to the window, but rested my thighs against the windowsill. "I would rather you still considered me your friend."

"I do, but now you're a friend who can boss me around." I groaned. Dom chuckled. "Relax, man. I can hear your teeth grinding from here. One day, your jaw will unhinge from the force."

"It's hard to relax where there's so much going wrong," I confessed.

A beat passed. "Want to talk about that?"

I shook my head. "How about you tell me something."

"What do you want to know?"

I shrugged. "About the town. About the people. About

yourself." I shrugged. "What are the people saying behind my back? Are they happy overall? Are they disappointed in me? Are you?"

Dom stared at me for a moment too long. "People seemed to be relieved you hadn't abandoned us as we thought you did." I almost winced. That statement still hurt me. Hurt them. "But they are anxious. Things haven't been easy. Everyone lost loved ones, the town is half-burned and half-broken, there are important positions in town missing, like ... even a hairdresser. We don't have someone to cut our hair anymore. Vianna is trying, but she has no training." He ran a hand over his messy mop. Now that he mentioned it, I could see his sideburns were slightly uneven. "When you think about it, it sounds silly compared with all the rest we're dealing with, but to them, that's life. That was their day-to-day. They can't move on without those."

I let out a sigh. "I can't suddenly revive the rest of the pack so they can take over their places. They are gone and we need to adapt. Some of us will need to learn new trades. For other things, we'll need to leave town to get it done, like a haircut, at least until time passes, the pack grows, more generations are born, and we can become self-sufficient again." That could take decades.

"I know. When I hear someone talking about It, I try squeezing myself into the conversation and making them understand that there's only so much we can do, and that you're definitely working overtime to provide for us all."

I nodded. "Thank you."

Dom frowned. "I'm sorry, man."

"For?"

"For this burden. I know you were trained to be alpha your entire life, but it was for a fully functioning town, with lots of people to help you through it. Also, the crystals were intact, the barrier was still up, and there wasn't a huge gap in the middle of town, and a creature who might wake up and come out at any time."

I scoffed. "Thanks."

"My pleasure," he teased.

I glanced back at the window right as Minsi and Rue were leaving the library. Minsi opened her arms and ran. I tensed a little bit—where the hell was she going? Then I saw it. Across the street, Raika walked out of the school. She ran toward Minsi. When my sister bumped into her, Raika pulled her up and spun her around. I could hear Minsi's happy squeal from here.

I couldn't help but smile.

"You like her," Dom said. I hadn't even noticed he had stood and was a foot behind me, looking out the window too. I wiped the smile from my face. "Even if you hide your smile, you can't hide it from me. I've known you since we were born, and I've known you've been into her for a long time."

"What?" I stared at him.

"The first time I realized it, we were about sixteen, I think. You had made up with Lucille about two months earlier, just to break up again. It was easy to see you're trying to force yourself to be with her. When you were with Lucille, you were so serious, so uptight. You almost never smiled. But then I saw the glint in your eyes when you looked at Raika and you thought no one else was watching."

My first instinct was to deny it, because that was what I would have done until one year ago. Because I had to protect Raika. But it was different now, wasn't it? If it depended on me, the entire world would know how much I loved her.

"Soon after, I realized that you never bothered her like we

did," Dom went on. "Quite the opposite, you protected her from us by creating other distractions, pointing out other things for us to do, and things like that. Then it became crystal clear."

"Who else noticed it?"

"Mace did." Our friend who died during the first battle. "However, knowing you liked her only made him want to hurt her more." He shifted his weight. "Me too, in the beginning at least."

I frowned, displeased with this confession, but it was good to have this out in the open now. "What about Lucille?"

"I don't think she knew. She never said anything, and I think she would have. No, she was too enamored with you to even consider you had your eyes on another girl."

I shook my head. "I should have been more careful."

"Don't worry. Mace and I only knew because we were the ones who spent the most time with you." He bumped his shoulder in mine. "So, will you tell me what's going on between you two, or should I make my own assumptions again?"

I snorted. There was no reason to keep this from him. Dom was my best friend. "Raika is my m—" I pressed my lips tight when I saw Serge and his friends strolling to the main square, toward where Raika and Minsi played tag.

"What does that old wolf want now?" Dom asked.

"Good question," I snarled.

My instinct was to go down there and stop him before he even opened his mouth and insulted Raika, but once again, I had to remind myself that I shouldn't do that. If I defended her in public, people would wonder what was going on, and Serge would definitely create a ridiculous story and start spreading across town.

"He and Lonan really give her a hard time, you know?" Dom said. "Raika did all she could for us, and yet, they never appreciated her. They never stopped bullying her, even from behind bars."

Raika saw Serge and the others coming and stopped playing. She gently pushed Minsi behind her and toward Rue, who was seated on one of the stone benches lining the paths in the main square.

Serge pointed his finger right in her face and yelled at her. I couldn't hear his words, but I heard the bite in them. Dear moon, my body thrummed with the need to pound his face.

Raika stood still. She spoke to him without raising her voice.

Serge turned to his friends, who stood a couple of feet back, laughed, then poked Raika on the shoulder. She took a step back.

And I did too, ready to go there and break his hand.

Dom put a hand on my shoulder. "Calm down. She's a big girl. She can handle him."

Serge yelled at her. Minsi yelled back. She jerked free from Rue's grip, ran to Raika, and shouted something at Serge.

He turned his enraged eyes to her and yelled right in her face. He raised his arm—

Raika planted her hands on his shoulders and pushed him back.

Minsi's shout turned into a scream. She pressed her hands to her ears and curled into herself. Raika turned to her. She embraced Minsi and the two of them crouched down together.

I growled. "That's it."

I ran from my office.

This time, Serge hadn't just harassed Raika. He had harassed Minsi, an eleven-year-old girl who was too little and frail for her age, and who everyone knew had panic attacks.

And she was having one now, because of him.

I didn't stop running until I was in Serge's ugly face—he reeked of beer. I shoved him back hard, making him stumbled several feet. He promptly straightened and snarled at me.

"What the—?" I clenched my hands as the Shadow Wolf made itself known inside of me. I could feel myself losing control. Dom hooked his arm around mine and held me back before I pummeled Serge's face. "What do you think you're doing?"

Serge stared at me, not caring who I was in the pack. "Your father would be ashamed of who you've become. Associating with filth, letting the trash play with your little sister." He spat on the ground, in Raika's direction. I lunged at him, but Dom stopped me once again. This time, Vallin had to help him. Serge chuckled. He was loving this.

I glared at him. "I made it clear that no one disrespects Raika. She has done more for this pack than any of us combined, and because of that, she isn't the omega." I moved my shoulders, freeing myself from Dom and Vallin. "But Raika can defend herself. I'm here, doing my best not to break your nose, because you scared my sister."

He glanced at Minsi, still in Raika's arm, shaking uncontrollably, while Raika whispered soothing words in her ear. "Like I said, you're all associating with filth."

I went for him again. This time, Dom and Vallin had trouble holding me back. This time, Serge had the decency of looking scared, even for a second.

This time, Raika spoke up. "Shane, he's not worth it."

He snickered. "Don't talk to me, omega."

"I'm not talking to you!" she snapped. "You're the one going out of the way to harass me!"

My Shadow Wolf stirred again. "Exactly." I faced Serge, my eyes deadly. "Last warning. Stop harassing Raika, or anyone else. Learn respect, use it. And learn how to be a part of a *pack*. You're not just one here doing what you wish. But, if that's what you want, I can make it come true. If I hear of you bothering Raika or anyone else in this pack, you'll be banished."

Serge's eyes rounded and stayed like that for several seconds. "You can't do that."

"Try me and you'll find out what I can or can't do," I snarled. "Now, put your tail between your legs and walk away before I break your nose."

Serge seemed like he wanted a fight, but when Dom and Vallin stood tall beside me, he huffed and left, his goons following him. I watched as he retreated and only relaxed when he was over a hundred yards from us.

Then I turned to Raika and Minsi and stood right by their side. I stared at them, at a loss for what to do. Minsi shook a little less, but she still had her face buried in Raika's chest. Raika stared up at me.

"Are you okay?" I asked, my fingers itching to reach for her.

She nodded. Slowly, she pushed to her feet and brought Minsi with her. My sister had a death grip around Raika's waist. "She'll be fine. Just give us a minute." Raika glanced down at Minsi and offered her a gentle smile. "Hey, sweetheart. Will you help me? I need to find five things you can see." Minsi's eyes darted around, her breathing ragged. Minsi didn't speak, but her eyes settled on five things for a couple of seconds. "That's great. Now how about four things you can touch?"

On she went with the countdown. I had never heard about it until Raika taught me the first time Minsi had a panic attack in front of me.

The anger toward Serge took a backseat to the gratitude I felt for Raika right now. Despite Serge being in her face and speaking hateful things, she had stood her ground and protected my sister. And it hadn't been the first time. Raika had done more for my siblings than I had.

And for that alone, my heart belonged to her.

I stood still, waiting as Minsi's breathing slowed and she stopped shaking. Rue was a few steps back, as tense as I was.

"How about we go bake a carrot cake?" Raika asked Minsi. "You like those, don't you?" Minsi nodded. Raika glanced at Dom, Vallin, Roman, then at me. "Can I use your kitchen?"

"I know why you're asking, and you know my answer," I said, my voice low, though I was sure the others could hear me, even if they were several feet back.

She lifted one shoulder. "Better safe than sorry." She started turning with Minsi.

I touched her arm, just for a second, before I pulled my hand away. "Thank you."

She offered me a closed smile. "Anything for her." Her eyes said more than that, and it was all I could do not to embrace and kiss her right here, right now.

She took three steps, then stopped, her face serious.

I followed her line of sight and saw Jay running out of the infirmary. I stiffened as he stopped in front of our group and said, "S-Shane, you have to see this."

19

SHANE

"You too, Raika," Jay said. "P-please."

I frowned. Why did Jay need Raika and me? I nodded and followed Jay back to the infirmary. Behind me, I heard Raika tell Minsi to go with Rue, that she would meet them at my house and bake the cake together.

Minsi whined but didn't give Raika a hard time.

Raika and I entered the infirmary, crossed the empty lobby, and walked in the back room, where a dozen beds lined the walls in a large room, and one of them was occupied. Dom and Vallin stayed outside.

Hamill, a middle-aged wolf and council member, who still had some spunk and was an exceptionally good fighter. During training, he showed impressive stamina. But now, in bed, he looked frail and weak, his skin was pale, and his eyes sunken in.

Jay approached his bed.

I followed him. "What's going on?"

Jay glanced at me and immediately lowered his gaze. "I-I'm not sure."

"What do you mean?"

Jay twisted his hands. "H-he started feeling ill this morning. Headache, blurred vision, a little fever." He looked at Raika and she nodded at him, a reassuring smile over her closed lips. "I-I thought he was coming down with a cold. We're not used to the weather and nature without the barrier. Even with our enhanced biology, we might feel the effects of that." True, I had been thinking a lot about that lately. "B-but later he came back and showed me his black fingers." Jay pointed to Hamill's hands, resting beside his body.

The tips of his fingers were pitch black. I had never seen anything like this before. "Tell me you know what is causing this?"

A trembling grin appeared across Jay's lips for one second. "Y-yes, I think so." He glanced at Raika once more. "I ran some tests and it seems it's some kind of magical poison." My gaze found Raika. Oh, no. "B-but I've never seen this kind of poison before."

"I can text Lavinia and ask her to stop by," Raika said, her tone dejected. She picked up her phone. "I think that if this is poison, they will be able to tell." She texted something fast and three seconds later her phone dinged. "Oh, they're still at the library and coming this way."

I nodded, my gaze falling back to Hamill.

First the land, now the wolves. If this was the same poison from the crystals, we would know what was causing it, but how could we make it better? How could we make it stop?

What if more wolves fell ill?

We stood in silence as Jay fussed over Hamill, checking his vitals every three seconds.

Not five minutes later, the infirmary's door opened and Lavinia and Almae walked in.

"We're here," Lavinia said, her gaze darting from side to side. When she saw Hamill, her eyes widened for a moment. "What is it?"

"Can you keep an eye on him?" Raika said to Jay, her tone sweet. Again, she offered that same soft smile.

Jay's cheeks gained a slight pink hue as he nodded.

Raika glanced at me, and together, we met Lavinia and Almae, away from Jay.

"He trusts you," I whispered to her.

"I know, and I don't know why."

"You took care of him and the others for an entire year. That probably affected some more than others. Jay is a nice guy, but he's insecure. He was looking for your approval."

She narrowed her eyes at me. "You aren't jealous of that, are you?"

I shook my head. "Not much. I am proud, though. You're already doing a great job as the alpha's mate."

Raika rolled her eyes at me.

I would have teased her more but we halted in front of Lavinia and Almae.

"We think it's the poison from the crystals," Raika said, going directly for the jugular.

Lavinia gasped.

"Oh, no," Almae said.

"Could you make sure it is the same poison?" I asked.

Lavinia nodded. "Of course."

"If it is, what else can you do?" Raika asked.

"We can try making a potion to delay the spread," Almae answered. "Maybe something for pain too, if it hurts."

"These damn crystals." Lavinia tsked. "If only we could take them out."

"We can try taking them out again," Almae suggested.

"But if we can't, we can try using them to make an antidote right where they are."

Lavinia's eyes widened. "Right. Why didn't I think of that?"

"Because I'm older, wiser, and I've seen my share of problems." Almae turned her kind eyes to me. "But Shane, if this is really caused by the crystals and we can't stop it, you might have to consider moving the pack to a safe location."

A growl started deep in my chest. This was my fucking home. I had been born and raised here. We all had. And we had fought for it and saved it from Conri. We were fixing it, making it better.

The idea of abandoning this town hurt almost as much as not being able to use the crystals anymore. As letting the barrier go.

As disappointing my people.

"No," I said through gritted teeth. "I won't think about that yet. We'll find some other way. We have to."

I marched out of the infirmary's back room and almost ran into Dom. Vallin was outside, waiting for orders.

"What is it?" Dom asked.

"Come on," I told him.

We walked out the infirmary. Vallin didn't even ask what was going on, he just walked with me as I headed toward the main square.

Roman walked out of the school and I pointed at him. "You. Come help."

"What is it?" Roman asked as he jogged toward us.

I halted in front of a trap door. Underneath it, one of the depleted crystals lay, quietly spreading its poison.

"We need to take these crystals out," I said.

Dom frowned. "But ... we just got them back."

He didn't know about the land, about Hamill, but I couldn't help my anger. I glared at him. "We are taking them out."

His frown deepened, but he nodded.

I opened the trap door and knelt before the crystal. I looked at it. At first glance, it seemed the exact same from before, but now that I knew it wasn't, I could see it. A black sliver swirling inside it, so faint, it seemed to disappear every few seconds. And then I found it again.

A fist clutched my chest, making it hard to breathe.

It had been so easy to find Dixon, to kill him, to get the crystals back. I should have known there was a plan behind all of this, a plan I didn't understand, a plan I was too busy to consider.

Didn't Nortrix say Conri was an errand boy? Someone was behind all of this, someone else, someone more powerful, crueler. Because if a powerful person wanted to destroy us, why not come and face us while our numbers were low and we were practically defenseless?

A cruel person didn't just barge in and destroy.

A cruel person played with his victims.

When I got my hands on this person—and the moon helped me, I would—I would make him suffer too.

Above us, the sky rumbled, the clouds darkening more.

I closed my hand around the crystal.

A jolt coursed through my arm, like a strong electrical surge, and I flew back a couple of feet, landing on my back.

Groaning, I rolled to my side.

Dom ran to me, offering me his hand. "Are you okay?"

"Yeah." The shock had faded, but my heart pumped against my rib cage. I could still feel the electricity running through me.

"What the hell was that?" Vallin asked when I knelt before the crystal again.

"That means this is going to be hard." I glanced up at them. "Go find some tools, rubber gloves, whatever we can use to pry these crystals from here."

Dom, Vallin, and Roman nodded and disappeared from my sight.

I reached for the crystal again.

The same jolt hit me, but this time I was prepared for it. I braced myself, gritted my teeth, and only skidded back a foot or two.

I ran a hand down my arms, my skin still electrified.

Fat drops fell down from the sky. Just what I needed when being electrocuted by a powerful, poisoned, magical crystal.

Cursing, I knelt beside the trap door again.

This was going to be a long night.

20

RAIKA

I ALMOST HAD A FIT WHEN I WALKED OUT OF THE INFIRMARY and found Shane, Dom, and Vallin taking turns trying to pry the crystal from its vault—in the rain!

I called Killian and asked him to help me make them see reason. To be fair, the others seemed relieved when I called it quits, but Shane was tenser than ever.

I sent them home—they didn't seem to mind receiving orders from the omega, didn't even question it—and I told Shane to go home too.

"I'll be there soon," I promised.

By the time I had taken a shower, changed into clean clothes, and gotten the ingredients I needed for tonight, the rain had stopped. For now. The clouds covered the sky, hiding the setting sun, and they rumbled every few minutes, promising more rain in the future.

When I got to Shane's house, he was in the shower. Tyren, who had opened the door for me, told me Shane had come back from a run.

"To clear his head," Tyren mocked.

An urge to go into Shane's bathroom and join him hit me, but Tyren stared at me as if he expected something, and Minsi was now attached to my waist. I couldn't get rid of them even if I tried.

And truth was, I didn't want to.

I loved Shane, but I loved his siblings too. In the future, when this mess was resolved, our people accepted me, and Shane told everyone I was his mate, the four of us would be a family.

My heart burst with that prospect.

While Shane was upstairs, I started dinner and made the carrot cake with Minsi. She helped me set the table in the breakfast nook, and Tyren sank on the couch in the family room and watched a superhero movie.

I had put the chicken pot pie and the carrot cake in the oven when Shane entered the kitchen from the mudroom. I turned to him with a smile, but that faded and my breath caught. He wore gray sweatpants and a fitted black shirt that molded to his hard chest and strong shoulders. He was barefoot, his hair was damp, and now I noticed the fine stubble covering his chin and jaw, as if he hadn't shaved in a day or two.

My heart sped up.

But then I saw and felt the tension in the knot between his brows, in the rigidness of his movements.

"I thought you had gone for a run to clear your mind."

He crossed the kitchen and halted right in front of me. "I did, but it didn't help."

I reached for him, then lowered my hands. Tyren knew about us, but what about Minsi? I didn't want to scare her. It was one thing to have me as a friend, but her brother's mate? That might spike her anxiety and give her a panic attack.

I glanced at her. She offered us an I-know-what's-going-on smile before sneaking into the family room and sitting beside Tyren with a book in hand.

I almost smiled too, but my mind was now on Shane. "Talk to me."

He leaned back on the counter beside the oven and crossed his arms. "We've spent hours trying to take the crystals from the damn vaults, and nothing worked."

I nodded. It had been stupid of them to even try. Lavinia and Almae had tried before, with brute force and magic, and it hadn't worked. Using shovels, screwdrivers, and whatnot wasn't going to do the trick. But I knew Shane had to try. He had to get it out of his system. It meant he was doing something, being proactive instead of waiting for the worst.

"You're doing everything you can," I said.

"My everything is not enough." His jaw hardened. "I tallied up everything that's going on right now that I can't fix. The crystals, the barrier, the poison, the dragon, the attack yesterday and Nortrix's threat this afternoon, and the fact that Conri might be a pawn in a bigger plan and someone is messing with us." He sighed and told me about his meeting with the alphas.

"That's not good," I said, my voice low.

Shane shook his head. "Perhaps Nortrix wanted to get in my head and make me feel worse. If that was the case, he succeeded."

I inhaled deeply. Yeah, the cards were stacked against us. And there was one more bit he either had chosen to forget, or he hadn't mentioned on purpose: my lineage and my newly awoken powers. Lavinia and Almae had given me a suppression potion I was supposed to drink every few hours, but could I do that for the rest of my life? Shouldn't I woman up and face the truth?

When listing everything like that, it felt like we were doomed.

I leaned into him, my head on his shoulder, my hand over his crossed arms. "I believe in you."

He scoffed. "At least one of us does."

"Shane …" I lifted my head and looked at him. "You're not alone in this. I'm here for you. Killian, Lavinia, Dom, Vallin, Rue … so many others. The entire pack. If it comes to that and you explain how dire the situation is, I know the pack will unite. We'll fight everyone and everything, and we'll win." The words came at me, and even though I probably needed a push to believe them myself, I felt inspired at the moment. I rose on my tiptoes and placed a kiss on his cheek. "Because I choose to believe in us."

He turned his face to me. "You're too good for me. By the moon, you're too good for the entire pack. We don't deserve you."

I rolled my eyes. "I don't like it when you say that. I don't feel like that, and when you say that, I feel like I have to live up to this perfect image of me you created in your mind."

Shane turned his body to me and placed his hands on my waist. "Just keep being you, do your thing, and I guarantee, this perfect image of you in my head won't ever change." He lowered his head and touched his lips to mine. I melted into him.

But I felt too self-conscious with his siblings in the other room, so I kissed him for three seconds, before the heat and desire overtook me, and I stepped back.

Shane locked his arms around my waist. "Where do you think you're going?" The oven dinged. He chuckled. "Saved by the bell." He pressed his lips to mine one more time before letting me go.

He called the kids to the table, and I grabbed the chicken pot pie from the oven. Then I sat down at the table with the three of them, and despite all the odds against us, I felt happier than ever.

DURING DINNER we played I-spy-with-my-little eye, and afterward, we stayed at the table playing Uno. Even Minsi participated, though she said only a handful of words the entire time. Still, the huge smile on her face warmed my heart.

But most of all, I was relieved Shane seemed a little better, a little less heavy. He even smiled a few times, and cracked a joke here and there. When Tyren tried cheating at Uno, as if that was even possible, Shane pulled him into a wrestling match, and Minsi and I pretended to be cheerleaders—for Tyren, of course.

We made chocolate frosting for the carrot cake and ate it as dessert. Everyone had second helpings.

Afterward, Shane helped me clean up while Minsi read a book in the living room, and Tyren went to his bedroom to play video games, no doubt. The way we moved in the kitchen, how we worked together to rinse the dishes, load the dishwasher, clean the counters, was like we had been doing it together for ages.

It was so easy to forget all the problems we faced, but it was also the break we needed. We couldn't just go, go, go and never rest, never take a breather. We needed moments where we were just a girl and a boy in love, spending time together.

Enjoying each other.

Later, I put Minsi in bed, stuck my head inside Tyren's bedroom to bid him goodnight—he just waved at me, his attention on his monitor—and headed to the front door.

Shane slipped his hands in his sweatpants' pockets and stared at me. "You know you don't have to go. They both know about us. They approve and want you here."

And I was grateful for that. But that wasn't all. "You know I can't stay. This is already too risky. If someone were to talk to you, they would see me here. If I spent the night and someone finds out, then it'll add to our list of problems." I gestured to the door. "Are you walking me out, or should I leave on my own?"

Looking like a puppy in the rain, Shane dragged his feet to the door. He opened it for me and stood under the door-jamb, blocking my way. "You know what? I don't think I'll let you go."

I chuckled. He was too cute for his own good. I walked to him, placed my hands on his hard chest, and pushed him back. Shane took two steps back onto the front porch, but placed his hands over mine, locking them in place. I tried pulling them back, but he wouldn't let them go.

"Why, you ..." I rose on tiptoes, intent on biting his chin, but he lowered his head and pressed his lips to mine. In a swift movement, Shane spun us around, pressed my back against the wall, and his body against mine.

I gasped against his mouth, and he took advantage of it to deepen the kiss.

All conscious thought fled my mind.

Shane adjusted himself, molding more of his body around mine, and I felt his hard-on pressing against my belly.

By the moon, I wanted him. I really wanted him, and I

had half a mind to tell him to rip my clothes off and have me right here.

Shane's hands slid down from my waist to around my ass. He pulled me up and his length rubbed right where I needed him. These damn clothes … they needed to be gone!

His mouth drew a fiery line across my cheek and he whispered, "One day soon, we'll do it against the wall."

I gasped, delirious with the possibility.

My place. He could come to my place with me. He could be careful and leave after and be back here without anyone seeing. Yes, my place. We would go to my house. Right now, before I combusted here. "Let's—"

Shane stiffened.

I was about to ask what happened when I heard it too.

Footsteps.

I snapped my head toward the source and inhaled sharply.

Lucille halted in the middle of the driveway, coming toward Shane's house. She stared at us with her jaw slackened as if we were two aliens.

"Shit," Shane muttered. He turned toward her. "Lucille—"

She whirled on her heels and took off.

My gut clenched. "Oh, no."

Shane ran a hand over his hair. "Shit," he repeated.

"I should go after her," I said, turning toward the entrance. "I need to talk to her before she tells anyone else."

Shane wrapped his hand around my wrist and pulled me back. "Wait. She won't tell anyone."

I stared at him. "Are you sure?"

He nodded. "I know her. She'll be pissed right now; she won't even want to see you. Me neither." He let out a sigh. "Give her some time. I'll talk to her tomorrow."

I frowned. It was true, Shane knew her better than I did. They had been friends since they were kids, and they had even dated for a couple of years. Though she and I had come to a truce when the pack was enslaved, I knew she wasn't a big fan of mine.

It felt like we had added another problem to our long to-solve list.

"I should go before anyone else sees us," I said, dejected. Did this mean Shane and I would have to be even more careful? That we couldn't even sneak out here and there? I didn't want to think about it.

"Hey." Shane pulled me closer. "You're more important to me than anything else, you know that, right?" He cupped my face. "Even if Lucille told everyone now and for some insane reason they all came with pitchforks, I would stand by your side. Forever."

"Hopefully, it won't come to that." I pressed a soft kiss on his lips. "Good night, Shane."

He held on to me for three more seconds, then finally he let me go. "Good night."

Lightning cut through the sky above my head and a rumble followed.

What I needed. To be rained on.

I hurried my steps and made it back home as the rain started again, stronger this time.

21

RAIKA

IT RAINED ALL NIGHT. I KNEW THAT BECAUSE I DIDN'T SLEEP well. I kept having nightmares of Lucille telling everyone about Shane and me. The pack turned against me and did horrible things—burned me at the stake like a witch, threw me off a cliff, tied stones to my bound feet and threw me in a deep river ...

It was insane.

Even if they didn't approve, no one would kill me.

Restless, I started my day earlier than usual. I went to the library, where books about poisons and crystals were spread over several tables, and delved into research. I didn't believe we would find anything in these books, but I was afraid of pushing them aside and missing something important.

Every fifteen, twenty minutes, I got up and glanced out the windows. I hoped to spot Lucille so I could talk to her. But so far, I had seen only a handful of people.

The rising sun peeked from the few breaks in the dark clouds—it seemed it wouldn't rain anymore today—and one patch cast light over the crack in the main square. Sometimes it felt ludicrous that there was a freaking dragon sleeping beyond the crack.

I frowned.

Curious about dragons, I weaved through the bookshelves until I found the mythical creatures section. Mythical was a loaded term, being that, to humans, even wolf shifters were mythical, but I hadn't been the one who organized these shelves!

I spotted a handful of books about dragons, wyrms, and wyverns. I picked them all up, found an empty table, and spread them around.

I didn't know much about dragons, but I was about to find out.

All of the books said basically the same thing: Dragons had come from another realm and were the most powerful of all supernatural beings. They were hunted by all because of their powers, and soon became extinct. Dragons weren't rational like humans or wolf shifters, and acted like predators, attacking anyone who got too close. They were hoarders and liked living inside dark caves, but they also liked the sky, especially at night. Most could breathe fire and all of them were impervious to flame.

Despite common belief, dragon shifters weren't born of a love story between a human and a dragon—ew—but of magic. The legend went that long ago, a human saved a powerful dragon. The dragon gifted the human with dragon magic, and thus the first dragon shifter was born.

Dragon shifters revered dragons and took care of them. When others hunted dragons, dragon shifters responded in kind. However, when the other shifters discovered that dragon shifters were as powerful as a dragon, they hunted them and the dragon shifters' numbers dwindled.

It had been centuries since dragons or dragon shifters had been seen, thus giving birth to the theory that both were extinct.

I glanced at the window in the distance. There was a damn dragon right here. Who said there weren't more dragons and dragon shifters out there too?

The greed of any being with a conscience was ridiculous. Why couldn't we all share this world and live in peace?

I heard voices coming from outside and went to the window. There she was. Lucille and Dom carried boxes into the infirmary—the shipment of medicine and other supplies. It was supposed to arrive early this morning.

I ran out of the library and had to skid to a stop in front of the infirmary when Lucille walked out again.

"Oh," she said, eyeing me up and down. "It's you."

Shit. "Can, hm, can I talk to you?"

Dom walked out a second later. He glanced at us, then continued moving toward the truck parked along the sidewalk. He picked up another box and carried it inside the infirmary.

Lucille stared at me. "Sure."

We walked to the edge of the main square and I turned to her. Once upon a time, Lucille had been my bully. Then she became an ally, trying to free the pack.

Now, what would she be?"

I shifted my weight. "Lucille, I—"

"I know," she said, forcing air out.

I frowned. "What do you know?"

She glanced around and lowered her voice. "That you and Shane are mates. I could tell from the moment I saw you two." She snorted. "Honestly, I look back now and I see it all there. The way he never engaged when we teased you."

Teased was a light word for what they did to me, but I wouldn't stop her now. "In fact, he often tried distracting us with something else. I remember I often caught him staring at you and I thought he was either pitying you for being the omega, or planning to terrorize you." She flinched at her own words. "He might not have known back then, but deep down, he knew. You know?"

I nodded. "I'm sorry," was all I could say. "I swear I always thought you would end up with him."

"Me too," she whispered. "Even though the mating bond never snapped for us, I hoped he wouldn't find his mate, I wouldn't find mine, and we would be happy together." She offered me a tight smile. "But he found his mate."

"I'm sorry," I repeated. "I just ... I know you're hurt, but Shane and I, we don't want others to know yet, so please, if you can—"

"Don't worry, I won't tell anyone." She waved me off. "I'm not stupid. I know that outing you both now will only make the pack turn against him, and that's the last thing I want. I might be hurt, but I can't hate him."

"You're reacting better than I would," I confessed.

She snorted. "Look, last night, I was ready to scream bloody murder, but I would like to think that this past year changed me. That I grew a little, that I matured. And that means facing what life throws at you with a brave face."

"Wow. Impressive."

"Don't tease me," she said. "I'm still hurt. I'll need time to digest this, but yeah ... you're okay. You look good together, actually." She paused, her lips pressed tight, then she finally said, "If I'm being honest, you're perfect for him. You worked harder than anyone else would to keep the pack safe last year. I know that if it weren't for you, things would have been much worse. Many more of us would have been killed."

My eyes brimmed with tears. "It was desperate times. Many people would step up and do more than they believe they would."

"Maybe, maybe not." She nodded at me. "Don't worry. Your secret is safe with me."

"Thank you. Your words, your trust, your secrecy. It all means a lot to me."

A dark gray wolf pounced toward us.

I pulled Lucille behind me, but then the wolf skidded to a stop and shifted right in front of us.

"Raika," Tyren said, breathless. "It's Minsi."

IN THE DISTANCE, Shane carried a limp Minsi to the infirmary. My heart sank.

Tyren shifted back and ran into the infirmary. I ran after him.

When I got there, Shane hovered over Minsi in a bed in the back of the infirmary. Tyren held a bedsheet around his waist, and Jay stood beside him.

"What happened?" I asked, my legs growing weak at the sight in the bed. Pale and sticky skin, sunken eyes, frail mien, and black-tipped fingers. I pressed a hand to my mouth. "Oh, no."

I leaned over the bed and ran my hand over Minsi's face, her skin hot against mine. Her eyes fluttered open, a faint smile spread over her lips, and then she went back to sleep.

Oh, my heart.

Shane's desperate eyes met mine. "She didn't come downstairs for breakfast. I thought she was being lazy and I let her be. I had some things I could do from home, so I worked there." His voice broke. "I should have checked on her earlier."

I walked up to him and slipped my hand into his, not caring who saw us now. "It wouldn't have changed anything." It was harsh, it hurt, but it was the truth. If he had found her earlier, it wouldn't have changed the fact that she was now the second victim of the crystal's poisoning.

"I-I'll give her some of Lavinia's potion," Jay said. He hobbled away from the bed and disappeared into a side door, where the supply room and restrooms were located.

"Is there anything I can do?" Lucille asked. She stood at the door.

"If you can, don't let anyone but Killian, Lavinia, and Almae enter," Shane said. She nodded. "Thank you."

With another nod, Lucille left the room and closed the door behind her.

I watched as Minsi's breathing grew ragged, her chest rising and falling quickly. Anger lashed through me. It was clear someone was toying with us. And I wanted nothing more than to get my hands around his—

And what? I couldn't even kill a Whitecrest wolf a couple of days ago. In my entire life I had only killed once and it had been a demon who was set on killing me, who had killed my mother and dozens of other wolves in our pack.

I didn't regret killing Phell, but the idea of killing again made me queasy.

Tyren sat on the bed, now wearing hospital scrub pants. He looked at his sister. "Why her?"

"I wish I knew." Shane's chest rumbled with a suppressed growl. "I spent hours touching the damn poisoned crystal yesterday and it didn't affect me." He touched her arm. "If I could, I would trade places with her."

I would too. "It seems to be random, but as we can see, this will continue spreading. How's the land?"

"Another three feet taken," Shane said.

Tyren looked at us. "What do you mean?"

Shane's nostrils flared. "This same poison is killing the land."

Tyren's eyes rounded. "What? Are you serious? What ... what do we do now?"

It pained me to say it, but ... "Shane, I know you don't want to—I don't want to either—but we need to think about leaving. If we leave, the land might still die, but at least the people won't get sick." I looked at Minsi and my vision blurred with tears. "At least, no one else will."

Shane's jaw ticked and his eyes hardened. He thought for a moment. This was clearly weighing on him. "I'll think about it."

22

RAIKA

SHANE AND I STAYED BY MINSI'S SIDE FOR HOURS. JAY GAVE HER the potion that supposedly delayed the poison's spread and helped with the pain. Lavinia and Almae came to check on her, and also on Hamill. Killian came to check on Shane, report, and receive more orders.

Shane was in no mood for orders, and he told Killian to do what he thought was right and be done with it.

Tyren went home for clothes and food, but came back with his tablet so he could sit beside Minsi and play video games.

I left for a couple of minutes, only to come back with a pile of books. "In case she feels better and wants to read something."

Shane shook his head. "Always the optimist—one of the many reasons I love you." I glanced around, afraid someone had heard him, but there was no one in here.

I settled the books beside Minsi's bed, but she had barely opened her eyes since she fell ill earlier this morning. I doubted she would be reading any books soon.

Rue came in near nightfall. She demanded Shane and I take a break while she watched over Minsi.

I had to pry Shane from Minsi's bedside.

Outside, Shane and I walked to the main square under the mostly cloudy sky. The rain was gone, but the chill remained. A wolf's blood ran hotter than a human's, and we didn't feel cold easily, but I wasn't used to any type of cold. I pulled my thin jacket tighter around myself.

Shane glanced down at himself. "If I had anything else other than my shirt, I would offer it to you. Unless you still want it. I can be shirtless, I don't mind."

"I don't mind either," I joked.

Shane offered me an I-see-what-you-did-there look.

We watched the trap doors, now closed again, and the trench cutting the square in half.

"I know leaving is the logical thing," Shane said. "But I still can't conceive of it."

"I know," I whispered. "This place is all we've ever known. And we just got it back. I can't imagine leaving either."

"But even if we find a way to stop the poison, we'll lose the crystals."

"If you want to stay, you can do what your father said. Ask witches to recreate the spell."

Shane looked at me. "You know I can't do that."

"Because of the dragon."

He nodded. "Because of the dragon."

It was cruel to have him down there against his will, sleeping for so long, buried in a dark hole alone. Someday, somehow, we would have to wake him, even though I had no idea how to take him out of there.

His brows knotted. "If we leave and let the poison take the land, won't that get to the dragon? Won't it kill him too?"

"I don't know. It's possible. I hate to say it, but we have to think of our people first. If you decide we should leave, I say let's take everyone to safety. Then we come back and figure out what to do with the dragon."

"We might need help for that."

"You made plenty of allies while you were with the DuMoir vampires. You can get us some help."

"True."

He was one call away from having the most powerful vampires and witches here. Then, why hadn't he called them already? If not for the dragon, then for the poison?

Shane grabbed his phone from his back pocket and stared at it. "I ... I need to do some thinking."

I understood. I couldn't begin to imagine how being alpha could weigh someone down. And ours was a broken pack, with many, many problems. To be honest, I wasn't eager for the day Shane told everyone about me and I became the official alpha's mate. Now, I moved with ease and almost no one paid me attention. When I became the alpha's mate, a weight would settle over me. Probably not as heavy as Shane's, but still more than I could bear.

"I'll go back to the library," I told him. "I still have lots of books to go through."

Shane nodded. "I might pick up some paperwork I need to look at and bring it to the library, so we can work together."

My first reaction was that wasn't a good idea. What if someone saw us working side by side? But I was getting tired of pretending and depriving myself of what I wanted to make sure the others got what they wanted. Besides, if anyone saw us, we could say I was helping the alpha with research. Which wasn't a lie.

I smiled at Shane. "I like that idea."

One corner of his lips curled up. "All right. I'll see you soon, then."

He turned and marched toward town hall, and I went to the library. Feeling a little lighter, I made some coffee in the backroom, filled two mugs, and went back to the largest table, where many of the books about crystals and poison were spread out.

I stared at the books for a second, my mind going back to all the bad things happening around us. I shouldn't feel lighter. I shouldn't feel a tiny bit better knowing Shane was coming to work beside me for a little while ... but I did. Hadn't I had this discussion with myself? I couldn't live in pain, agony, and frustration all the time. No one of us could. Here and there, we had to force some bright spots to shine through, otherwise we would succumb to the bad, fall so deep, we would never see the light again.

I shook my head, clearly delusional. When did I get so philosophical?

I sat on a chair at the table, set the mugs down, and picked up one of the books. A moment later, the front door opened and I smiled. But when I saw who entered, my blood chilled.

"Serge." I stood from the chair. "What are you doing here?"

Grinning like a fool, he walked toward me. Or rather, he traipsed. He tripped over his feet and laughed. Oh, shit, the man was drunk again.

"I'm here for payback, bitch," he said, his words slurred.

"Payback? What did I ever do to you?"

"You existed! The scum of the world. You got Lonan killed. You asked Conri to keep us enslaved." He narrowed his eyes. "Do you think I don't know you were in league with him? You always hated us. You were jealous of our status, of our power, so when the opportunity presented itself, you took it. You joined Conri and mistreated us."

I gaped at him. "You're delusional."

Serge stalked toward me. "All the misfortune falling on us now? It's all because of you. The moon knows that and once I kill you, everything will right itself."

I rounded the table, keeping it between us. "Serge, I don't want any trouble with you. Just walk away."

"No, no. Don't you see it? I have to kill you. Only then will all the bad karma around our pack end."

I shook my head. "That's ridiculous."

"Time to die, bitch." Serge lunged at me. He jumped over the table, surprisingly nimble for a man who looked a lot younger than he was.

I wiped the shock from my face and ran from him.

But I didn't get far. Serge's hand closed around a bunch of my hair and he yanked my head back. I yelped and lost my balance. Serge pushed me to the ground and I hit my head hard, my vision blurring.

He straddled me, his hands on my neck. "I almost shifted into my wolf for this, but I want you to see the joy on my face while I kill you."

I jerked under his grip and once again I was surprised by his strength. I punched his arms, I tried moving my hips to push him away, but he didn't budge.

Black spots clouded my sight. I would faint, and then there was no stopping him. Serge would kill me. That realization filled me with despair.

Darkfire awoke inside of me, and for the first time, I welcomed it. I held on to it with both hands and pulled. The darkfire filled my veins. With a groan that turned into a scream, I shifted one of my arms and swiped at Serge's face.

His head snapped to the side and he lost his balance. I rolled from under him and stood up. Serge pressed a hand to his face and rose to his feet. When he pulled his hand away, there was blood on his palm.

And two nasty scratches across his cheek.

"I'll kill you," he snarled. He grabbed the heavy books from the table and threw them me, one after the other. I blocked them with my arms, but one hit me in my eyebrow, and in a few seconds, a trickle of blood covered my left eye.

Serge rammed into me, pushing me back into a tall shelf. But I was brimming with darkfire. Shadows covered my arms and I pushed him away. Serge flew back, hit another shelf and slid to the floor, several books falling over him.

Blood rushing in my ears, I stalked to him. If he wouldn't leave me alone, then I had to end this. And there was only one way to do that.

I raised my shifted arm, intent on clawing his heart out.

"Raika!"

I snapped to attention and glanced toward the voice. Shane stood by the door, his eyes wide, his posture coiled. I gasped, as if waking from a dream, and the darkfire faded to background noise.

Serge pushed to his feet and snarled at me.

Shadows wrapped around Shane and his eyes turned red. Oh no. He rushed Serge, but I stepped in his path. "Shane, no." He bared his teeth at me. "Shane, don't let it win. You can control it."

Serge laughed. "Are you really going to listen to that whore?"

Faster than I could react, Shane sidestepped me and punched Serge. Holding his nose, the old wolf fell on his ass.

Shane took a deep breath. His eyes returned to normal and the shadows were nowhere to be seen. "I warned you and now you give me no choice. Serge, you're banished. You've got one hour to pack and leave. I don't care where you go, just *leave!*"

Serge stood, his nose bleeding. "I'm not going—"

The shadows came back with full force. Fur covered Shane's arms and red shone bright from his eyes. He wrapped a claw around Serge's neck and lifted him up clean from the floor. "You'll go," Shane said, his voice deeper. Not his own. "Or I'll kill you and make an example out of you." He squeezed a little more. "Do you understand?"

Serge nodded slightly since he could barely move his head.

Shane opened his claw and Serge fell to the floor. He recovered quickly, glared at me once more, and then ran out of the library.

Shane stood there, half Shadow Wolf, half himself, breathing hard, his body hard with anger.

I stepped into his personal space and placed a hand over his heart. "Shane, look at me." Slowly, he turned his gaze to me, his eyes changing from red to brown every few seconds. "It's okay now. I'm okay. Come back to me."

With a deep breath, the red was fully gone, the fur disappeared, and the shadows left. His gaze fixed on my bleeding eyebrow and he cupped my face. "Are you okay?"

I nodded. "Other than this pesky scratch, I think so."

He smoothed my hair back. "I'm glad you were able to defend yourself."

"If you hadn't shown up, I think I would have used dark-fire. To hurt or to kill him, I don't know."

"If you hadn't stopped me, I would have let the Shadow Wolf take over, and I would have ripped him to pieces."

"I guess we make a good couple," I teased, trying to lighten the mood.

A lopsided grin spread over his lips. "The best."

Shane placed a soft kiss on my forehead. "Come on." He held my hand in his. "We need to clean that cut."

23

SHANE

I would have held Raika's hand as we crossed the main square to the infirmary, but she wouldn't let me.

Once inside, Jay fussed over Raika. I first had thought he had tremendous respect and admiration for her, for all she had done for the pack for the past year, but I was starting to think it was more than that. It might have started that way, but now as he helped her sit down on a chair and meticulously cleaned the cut, I was quite sure his feelings had evolved.

So besides Roman, I had to watch out for Jay too?

Thankfully, the cut above Raika's left eyebrow was just a nasty scratch. Jay cleaned it, applied some healing salve, and put on a thin bandage.

While he did that, I texted Dom, Vallin, and Killian and let them know about Serge's banishment. I probably should have used my alpha command on him, but I had been so out of it, with my Shadow Wolf almost taking over, I hadn't really thought of it. Dom texted back saying he would check on Serge and make sure he left within the hour.

I tucked my phone back into my pocket.

"All better," Jay said with a big smile. Funny how he didn't stutter when talking to Raika. Was I that intimidating, or was there something else? I was probably just seeing things.

"Thanks, Jay." She rose from the chair.

Since we were here, we checked on Minsi and Hamill again. They were still weak and unconscious, but they hadn't gotten worse in the meantime.

Rue shooed us away, saying our "time off" had barely started. "And you already managed to get in trouble." She shook her head.

Raika and I walked out of the infirmary again.

She halted on the sidewalk and looked around. There weren't many people around, still she lowered her voice when she said, "Aren't you afraid of the consequences Serge's banishment will have?"

"It'll serve as an example." My mood soured thinking of that damn wolf. "Disrespect isn't allowed in this pack. The bullying from when I was younger? That will be cut at the root if necessary. I waited years to be able to do that and I'm not going back."

"I'm proud of you for that, but I'm worried his friends will start something," she said.

"Then they will be banished too."

"We barely have any wolves left in the pack. If you banish more, then what will be left of us?"

"We don't need those kind of wolves in our pack."

"I agree, but maybe there's another way to solve this problem."

"Like what?"

Raika shrugged. "I don't know. I'm just ... I would rather

have a civilized talk and solve things that way than fights that end in banishment."

I could see her point, but wolves like Serge wouldn't. They were beyond reasoning. To them, a harsh and fast action was worth a thousand words.

The sound of a car approaching held my attention. Raika and I glanced to the same spot five seconds before an SUV came down Main Street. Killian was behind the wheel and—

"What the ... ?"

The SUV stopped beside us. With a grin, Killian climbed out. "Look who I found."

The passenger door and one of the backseat doors opened, and Evelyn and Ash spilled out.

"What the hell?" I finished my previous sentence. "What are you two doing here?"

I blinked. I hadn't seen them in six or seven months, since we ran from the Nightmist witches together.

Evelyn smiled at me. "You'll never believe us."

Ash grabbed my forearm tight. "How have you been?"

I tilted my head. "Could've been better." I stared at them for a second, then gestured to Raika. "Evelyn, Asher, this is Raika, my mate."

Raika's eyes rounded, as if she didn't expect me to tell them that. I hadn't spent a lot of time with Evelyn and Ash, but I knew Lavinia trusted them blindly, and that was good enough for me. "Evelyn and Ash helped Lavinia and Killian take down the Nightmist witches' lodge. That was when I was freed."

"Oh." Raika's face brightened. "Then I owe you thanks for saving him."

I scoffed. "You say that as if I was a damsel in distress and didn't do anything."

Evelyn cupped her mouth and whispered, "He didn't do anything."

"Hey!" I snapped.

Evelyn chuckled. "It's so nice to meet you, Raika." She had long, dark hair, smooth olive skin, and big chocolate eyes.

Ash waved at Raika. He was tall with light-brown hair, and blue eyes that rivaled Raika's. He glanced at me, one of his hands on the hilt of the long sword hanging from his hips. "I didn't know you had a mate."

I ran a hand through my hair. "Yeah, well. Until a month ago, I thought she was dead."

Raika winced, but her eyes met mine and a wave of gratitude filled me. In the craziness of our days, it was easy to forget how good it was to be here with her, even if we still played pretend when around others.

"And I thought he had been a coward and abandoned us," Raika said. Sweet revenge. I smiled at her.

"Ouch, that must have been hard," Evelyn mused.

Raika nodded.

I grimaced. "Can we change subjects? Go back to my first question? Like ... what the hell are you two doing here?"

"I felt a dragon's magic," Evelyn said. "It got stronger once we entered the town."

Right. Evelyn was a light witch with a dark witch's power—she could sense and absorb a dragon's magic. It was said that when a dragon died, their magic was stored in their bones. Evelyn went around finding dragon bones, to keep them away from dark witches. She kept them hidden, even from herself, since it was easy to lose her mind to the dark magic.

"Are you hiding dragon bones around here?" Ash asked, in a teasing tone.

I looked at Killian. "You didn't tell them?"

Killian shook his head.

"Tell us what?" Evelyn asked.

I gestured to the crack by our side. "There's a dragon sleeping in there."

Evelyn's eyebrows rose sky high. "No way."

I told them how the dragon ended up there. I also told them about the crystals, the poison, and the fact that it could be hurting the dragon too.

Evelyn paced, her eyes on the crack. "We need to get him out."

"I agree, but I don't know how," I said. "Since the crystals are the thing keeping him asleep, I think taking them out would do the trick. I can easily take two crystals out, but the other two are stuck."

She halted. "You said the crystals feed from the dragon's magic. I've never channeled from a live dragon before—they are supposed to be extinct—but I can try. I can try using his magic to repel the crystals. Maybe then, you'll be able to take out the two poisoned crystals."

"Evie," Ash said. "You know you shouldn't use dragon magic. Channeling directly from a dragon might be even stronger."

"I know, but what's the other option? Leave the dragon down there? I can't do that." She rested a hand on Ash's chest. "Besides, you know you have my permission to knock me out if I go berserk." They stared at each other for a minute, until Ash nodded his agreement. She looked at me. "Do you want me to try?"

I considered that. How would the dragon escape the

underground? The gap would widen, causing more damage to the town? Would there be another earthquake? "What can go wrong with the spell?"

Evelyn shrugged. "I don't know. Anything? I'm not really sure what we're dealing with here, and I've never attempted anything like this before."

"What if we free the dragon and it turns on us?" Raika asked.

Right, I had forgotten about that.

"It's a possibility," Ash said.

"If he attacks us, I can use my magic to deflect it," Evelyn said. "I can trick the dragon and guide him away from here. Isn't Lavinia here? She can help me with that."

Could it be worse than leaving the crystals in the vaults, having them kill the land and the dragon, and poison my people? Then us having to run away?

At this point, I was willing to try almost anything.

I let out a long breath. "Do it."

I THOUGHT Evelyn would simply stand there and channel the dragon's magic, and in two minutes it would have worked, or not, and we would be done.

But she called for Lavinia to gather supplies for the spell. Almae joined them. Meanwhile, Raika and I asked everyone to stay back. No one came within a hundred yards of the main square.

Rue stayed in the infirmary with Minsi, and we told Jay to be ready to flee with them. Tyren, who was still in the infirmary, wasn't having it. He said he would go where I went.

It was early afternoon when we finally gathered in the

square again—me, Raika, Killian, Lavinia, Evelyn, Ash, and Almae.

Evelyn, Lavinia, and Almae placed small, white crystals and smoking herb bunches on the ground around the trench. I opened the hatches where the crystals were hidden and stood by one of the poisoned crystals. Ash stood by the other one. When Evelyn told us to, we would reach for the crystals and take them out.

Raika and Killian stood with Tyren, Dom, and Vallin a hundred yards back. I had told them to keep an eye out. If anything went wrong ... well, I didn't want to think about that.

Raika had argued she wanted to be close in case she could help, but anything could happen and I had to count on her to protect my siblings.

"Ready?" Evelyn asked. Everyone either nodded or voiced their okays. "Here goes nothing."

Evelyn rolled her shoulders, closed her eyes, and extended her hands out over the trench A few seconds later, the crystals flickered and the herb bundles smoked. She muttered under her breath, words I couldn't understand. Her brows knotted and sweat gathered on her forehead. She grunted and splayed her fingers.

The crystals shone brightly nonstop, and the herb bunches caught fire.

Evelyn opened her eyes—they glowed green!

"I feel it," she whispered, her voice rough, almost foreign. "The dragon. He's sleeping, but he can feel he's in the pre-awake phase. He wants out." She gasped. "His power ... it's amazing."

Her hand glowed the same green as her eyes.

Lavinia and Almae placed their hands on Evelyn's shoulders and closed their eyes. Were they lending their magic to Evelyn? Whatever it was, they were helping her.

Evelyn gasped. "I'm doing it. I'm redirecting his magic." She gritted her teeth. "Be ready!"

A green light shone from underneath the crystal. I knelt beside it, ready to grab it. Even if it shocked me again, this time I wasn't going to let go.

The crystal hummed and trembled. "Evelyn?"

"I'm trying," she said, her voice strained. "Oh, the spirits, no!"

Green flashed from the vaults, from the gap. The crystal trembled again and melted into a goo of black. "No!" I cried, reaching for it. I touched the goo before it sank into the earth and hissed as it burned my fingertips.

I stared at the vault. The crystal was gone.

Was it a good or a bad thing?

"Evelyn!" someone yelled.

I turned and saw Evelyn faint, Lavinia and Almae holding her limp body. Ash ran to them and caught Evelyn in his arms. I stared from them back to the vault.

What had happened?

I shook my head. A person's life was more important than the crystals. I ran to them and joined Lavinia and Almae, who hovered over them. Raika, Killian, Tyren, Dom, and Vallin came closer too.

Ash knelt on the ground with Evelyn in his arms. He touched her face. "Evie? Talk to me."

Evelyn's eyes fluttered open. "I'm okay ... just tired."

"The spell took too much of your energy." There was a reprimand in Ash's voice.

I bit my lip, holding the questions inside. But Evelyn knew. She propped her head on Ash's shoulder and looked at me. "I couldn't do it. The dragon was fighting it. He didn't want me taking more of his magic. He was the one who sent that incredible burst. It fried our connection."

"And it melted the crystal," I said.

Evelyn's eyes rounded. "What?"

Ash nodded. "The crystal became a black liquid. It was absorbed by the earth."

"Oh no." Evelyn tried sitting up. "I'm so sorry."

I was pissed, but … "It's not your fault."

Raika gasped. "What if this messes up the land more?"

"On it," Killian said. He dashed away with his vampire speed.

I frowned. "What do you think happened?"

"I'm hoping that the dragon's magic obliterated the crystals," Evelyn said, her voice still weak. "If that happened, then the poison is gone and the dragon will awake fully and break through the ground. If not—"

"Shane!" someone yelled.

I turned to the voice.

Roman ran to us.

I frowned. "What is it?"

He halted ten feet from us and inhaled deeply. "Just … I don't even know how to explain it."

"Just say it," I said through gritted teeth.

"Lucille, Hugh, and Jena," he said. "All of a sudden, the three of them fell to the ground, their bodies, shaking. When we touched them, they were burning up. And now their fingertips are black."

My chest felt like it was being crushed by a boulder.

"No," Raika whispered.

Killian zoomed back. His eyes met mine and I knew. "Tell me," I said, my voice tight.

"It's spreading, faster than before," he said. "In the few seconds I was there, it advanced an entire foot."

No, this couldn't be happening.

The crystals hadn't melted and disappeared into oblivion. They had melted into poison and it was now spreading and killing faster.

There was only one option left.

24

RAIKA

EVEN THOUGH TIME WAS TICKING, WE MOVED SLOW. FIRST, Shane ordered the sick wolves to be brought to the infirmary. Jay, Lavinia, and Almae would look over them.

Second, Ash took Evelyn to the infirmary too—under her protests. Almae told her they would do a quick exam to make sure she was fine, that was all.

Third, Shane ordered everyone to remain calm and not tell the others what was going on just yet. He didn't want to start a panic. He said he needed a moment to gather his thoughts and would make an announcement.

He retreated to his office in the town hall and I went with him. There was no one else in the building, so I didn't bother closing the door.

Shane paced beside the desk, his face gaunt, his shoulders tense.

I stood by the door, giving him space. "Tell me what I can do for you?"

"Restore the crystals? Un-melt them? Recreate their magic?"

"Unfortunately, I can't do anything of that. No one can."

He groaned, halted, and looked at me. His hard eyes softened. "Sorry, I didn't mean to dump that on you. It's just …"

"I know. You're disappointed, upset, angry, hopeless. I feel like that too."

He nodded. "You were the alpha while I was gone. I know you care for the pack as much as I do, if not more."

"Shane …" I bit my lip. I had promised not to hide anything from him again, so I had to tell him. "Since the dragon's magic melted the crystals, I think it affected the others too, somehow."

"Why do you think that?"

I brought my hands up. "Because I can feel my demon half stronger inside me." I thought about it, and a swirl of shadow enveloped my fingers. Shane's eyes widened. I closed my hands into fists and the shadow disappeared. "Didn't the crystals keep the darkfire in check? When two were gone, I felt it awakening. Now I feel it even more."

"Shit. Is it bothering you? Do you feel out of control?"

I shook my head. "So far, it's okay. Just … there's more of it than before. I … with this mess, I forgot to tell you. Lavinia made me a suppression potion, to help control the darkfire until I have more time to learn to control it." Or I could keep drinking it forever … "I started this morning."

"And you still felt the darkfire grow stronger?"

I nodded. "I can ask Lavinia if it's okay to drink a bigger dose of the potion for now."

"It's one damn problem on top of the other. And you know what bothers me the most? The fact that someone is playing with us as if we were pieces on a chess board. Whoever let us have the crystals back knew something like this would happen. Maybe not with Evelyn and channeling the dragon's magic, but if we had called Thea and the Silverblood coven to help. Maybe that much magic would have melted the crystals and the poison would have spread sooner. This was all premeditated."

My brow furrowed. "Who would do that, and why?"

"Hell if I know."

"This is cruel."

"Agreed."

I embraced him. I felt the tension flee his body as he embraced me back. I lay my cheek on his chest. His heartbeat thudding against my ear.

"What do we do now?" I knew the answer. He knew the answer. But I wanted to hear him say it.

He pulled back and stared at me, a sadness shining in his eyes. "Now, we leave."

THE SUN WAS HALFWAY down the horizon and soon it would disappear behind the trees, though we still had about two hours until complete darkness. We gathered in the square.

Everyone was here—the wolves, the kids, the vampires, the witches. The only ones missing were those affected by the poison—they stayed in the infirmary with Jay. He was curious about what this was all about, but I gave him a hint. "Start packing."

It had been a couple of hours since the crystals melted, but two more wolves had fallen sick. If we didn't do this soon, all of us would fall ill.

Shane climbed over one of the remaining benches in the square, with Dom and Vallin on the ground beside him.

Killian, Lavinia, Evelyn, and Ash were nearby in case

something happened. Like the dragon bursting from the ground.

I wanted to be there with them, but I stayed back with Tyren, Rue, and Roman.

"Sorry to call you at this time of the evening," Shane started. "But I have urgent news that can't wait."

A murmur spread through the crowd. There weren't many of us left, but right now it sounded like a full stadium.

"Quiet!" Vallin snapped.

Silence fell over the square.

"Unfortunately, the crystals that once powered the barrier and supported the magic around our lands are gone," Shane said. "Two of them turned harmful. The sick people? That's because of the crystals." Murmurs began anew, but Shane didn't stop. "The crystals are also poisoning the land. As we speak, the poison is spreading through the forest around us and killing everything it touches. And ... it's heading this way."

"What are we going to do?" someone asked.

"Can we get new crystals?" someone else asked.

"There are witches here," someone said. "How about a spell?"

Rue leaned closer to me. Her eyes held a gleam of fear. "Did you know about this?"

Feeling awful for having hidden this from her, I nodded.

"We've tried all we could," Shane continued. "But I'm afraid there's nothing we can do for the land now. Because of that, I'm ordering everyone to return to their houses and pack the essentials, because tonight we're leaving town."

The murmurs increased to a full chatter, filled with terror.

"Just leave? We can't leave!"

"I won't leave my house!"

"I can't pack that fast!"

"Why not wait until tomorrow?"

Shane growled. "We can't wait until tomorrow, because it has been a little over two hours since the crystals were destroyed, and five more wolves are now sick. If we wait until tomorrow, how many more will get sick? Ten? Twenty? We can't risk it." The voices increased and Shane raised his hands. "All right, I'll say it again. Go back to your houses, pack what you can, and in two hours, we leave. Do it, or I'll use the alpha's command."

That seemed to shake everyone awake. The crowd started dispersing.

Serge hopped onto another bench and yelled, "I also have an announcement."

I stared at him. What was this crazy wolf doing?

"Serge, you're banished!" Shane snarled. "You shouldn't be here!"

"Oh, I know I was banished." The two scratches on his face looked ugly and raw even from here. "But I thought the pack should hear something important before I leave for good."

"There's nothing for you to say!"

"But there is." A wolfish grin took over his face. "You're all wondering why all of this is happening to us? Why our previous alpha was killed? Why we were enslaved by a half-wolf, half-demon? Why our current alpha is cursed? Why the land is dying? Why wolves are getting sick? I know the answer."

Now he had everyone's attention. Even mine.

"Serge, shut up!" Shane shouted. "You're banished! Leave or I'll make you leave."

The crowd spoke louder.

"We want to hear him!"

"Let him speak!"

"Wait! I want to hear his piece!"

Shane growled. I was sure he wouldn't hear the people, but Serge was faster. He pointed his finger at me. "It's because our alpha is mated to the omega!"

All faces turned to me. I sucked in a sharp breath. A new wave of murmurs started.

"He's mated to her?"

"She helped us, but I don't want her as the alpha's mate."

"The alpha likes her? Ew."

"But she's the omega!"

"She doesn't deserve this."

"She doesn't deserve him."

Tyren stepped in front of me, as if he could protect me from the harsh words.

Shane glared at Serge before turning to the crowd. "It's true Raika and I are mated," he said over the crowd. "But that's not the reason for the problems we're having."

Serge scoffed. "I can prove it is." He looked at me. "She's a whore, who was in league with—"

"Watch it!" Shane advanced on Serge, but Dom and Vallin held him back.

"—Conri. She's the one poisoning our land and our friends."

"What?" I asked, my voice faint.

"You know how? She's a half-wolf, half-demon like Conri!"

My throat went dry, the blood rushed to my ears. How ... how did he know this? Had he seen the shadows around my arms that day? No, he couldn't have. He had been down, covered in books.

Shane got rid of Dom and Vallin, but Serge had come prepared. His friends stood in his way, pushing Shane back.

"But, dear wolves, let's not despair," Serge continued. "I have a solution for this."

"Banish her!" someone yelled.

"Kill her!" another one added.

Now Roman held my wrist and pulled me several feet back. He was getting ready to run with me, but I yanked my hand from his grip. I wasn't going to run from this. This was ridiculous and the pack would soon see that.

Suddenly, Lavinia, Killian, Evelyn, and Ash stood beside me too.

"No need to kill her," Serge said. "Not yet." He laughed. "But we all agree our alpha isn't the right one for us. He left us. He stayed away for an entire year, not caring for us—"

"That's a lie!" Shane yelled, lost somewhere in the crowd. I could barely see the top of his head as he wrestled with Serge's friends.

I held on to Killian's arm and said, "Make Shane stop. Don't hurt Serge. He was already banished, fighting will make it worse. We have to solve this in a civil way, or people will think Shane's unhinged, and that won't help our cause."

Killian disappeared from my side. Three seconds later, I could see him pushing Shane back, talking to him. Shane fought him for a moment, then stopped. But the tension in his shoulders, in his expression, didn't ease.

"Our alpha is cursed," Serge continued. "In a handful of days, the full moon will be back and we'll have to lock him up so he doesn't kill us. What kind of alpha is that?" A roar of agreement came from the crowd. Oh, by the moon. "Moreover, he lost our crystals, and he's abandoning our land, without even fighting for it."

"That's not true!" Shane yelled once more. At least he had stopped advancing on Serge.

Slowly, Shane made his way toward me. As he weaved through the crowd, people glared at him, pushed him, cursed at him. But he ignored them all, his eyes set on mine.

He reached me, grabbed my hand, and pulled me to his side. Our friends surrounded us.

"Shane isn't fit to be our alpha!" Serge shouted. "Because of that, I invited someone who is." He gestured to one of the side roads.

What?

Slowly, we turned around. I gasped and gripped Shane's hand tighter.

Wolves with white spots on their fur surrounded us. I tried counting fast, but in front of us, I saw twenty. They closed a circle around the square, around all of us. There had to be at least a hundred here. That was twice our number.

If I took into consideration that we might have lost at least half of our pack to Serge and his speech, then it was even less than that.

A man walked forward from behind the wolves. Long blond hair, fair skin, and light blue eyes—the most common traits of the Whitecrest wolves. Unlike others here who wore normal or combat clothes, he had come in a light gray suit with a baby blue tie.

"Nortrix," Shane said with a growl.

Nortrix flashed Shane a triumphant smile. "Hi again. I told you we weren't done."

Growling, Shane took a step forward. I grabbed his arm with both hands and Killian extended his arm in front of Shane's chest, like a metal bar, blocking his way.

"What are you doing here?" Shane asked.

Nortrix took three steps forward, but kept a safe distance from us. "I could just come here and take over, kill you right here, right now, but I'm not that cruel. I want to give you a chance."

Shane bared his teeth. "I'll give you a chance. Walk away now or my friends and I will kill you and your wolves."

Nortrix laughed. "Look around you, Shane. What friends? The dozen around you? You know that's not enough. You also know this"—he gestured to his wolves—"is only a small part of my force. If I brought them all in here, you all would fall in five seconds flat."

"He's right," I whispered to Shane. "Calm down and listen to him."

Without breaking his hateful stare from Nortrix, Shane inhaled deeply. "What do you want?"

"A formal challenge. Tomorrow at sunrise. Meet me where we met last time." I sucked in a sharp breath. A challenge? "The winner takes it all. Both packs. And the packs will be bound to respect that."

Shane shook his head. "Why are you doing this? You have to know our numbers are small and our lands are dying. We were about to evacuate."

Nortrix nodded. "I know."

"Then why? What do you want?"

"That's my business." Nortrix's lips turned down. "Shane, I formally challenge you. Do you accept?"

Shane stiffened, his arm rock hard beneath my hands. "I do."

What? Was he insane? We were leaving, not fighting.

Nortrix nodded. "Very well. I'll see you tomorrow." He spun and walked away. One by one, his wolves broke formation and followed him.

Serge and his friends shifted and followed Nortrix. Another half dozen wolves did the same.

At least it wasn't the entire pack.

When they were all finally gone, the tension burst and voices filled the air. Questions, comments, insults, screams all floated around like cold wind in a storm.

"QUIET!" Shane said, using his alpha command. Every single one of us felt the command vibrate through us and we all quieted. The witches and the vampires weren't affected, but they too remained still. "Not you," he whispered to me. The rush came again, freeing me from his previous command.

"Thanks," I whispered back. I didn't like he had to do this, but I understood why.

Shane stepped over a ledge on the pavement and stood a head taller than most wolves. "I didn't want to use that, but you left me no choice." He shook his head once. "I don't care if you don't agree with me, if you hate Raika and me, if you're seriously questioning all of your life choices right now. The land is dying and wolves are getting sick. Everyone needs to leave tonight, even if it's just to run to the Whitecrest pack. Or become a lone wolf, or create your own pack. I truly don't care. What I care is that no one else is hurt by this mess. I'll release you from the command, and I won't issue another one. But please, do what I ask of you. Go home, pack, and leave. Tomorrow is another day, and we'll solve everything."

The thrum of magic coursed through the air and everyone started moving again. The wolves glanced at each other, talked, murmured, but after a few minutes, everyone walked away.

Everyone but us: me, Shane, Tyren, Killian, Lavinia, Evelyn, Ash, Almae, Dom, Vallin, and Roman.

Killian clicked his tongue. "What are your orders?"

"Escort everyone out and go with—"

"Wait," Dom interrupted him. "I know you. You'll tell us to leave and you'll stay to face Nortrix tomorrow." Dom clenched his fists. "The hell with that!"

"Dom," Shane started with a growl. "Please, don't test me. My mood is near to exploding right now, and I can even feel the forsaken Shadow Wolf trying to come out."

Dom pressed his lips tight.

"But ... we're still days from the full moon," I said.

"It seems I'm losing more and more control over him," Shane said. "Escort everyone out and to safety. Go to the nearest town, rent rooms at an inn for everyone. Hopefully tomorrow I'll join you all."

"And if you don't?" Tyren asked, his voice breaking.

My heart squeezed.

"If I don't ..." Shane inhaled sharply. "If I don't, then just do what Raika tells you to."

Tyren glared at Shane. Then he spun around and took off.

"Tyren!" Shane called out.

"Let him go," Killian said. "He won't listen to reason when he's angry. Just like someone I know." He looked at Shane.

Shane let out a long breath. "All right, people, everyone out. Now. Please."

Slowly, our friends moved.

I held Shane's hand as we watched them go, trying hard not to break down. What the hell had just happened?

25

SHANE

I DIDN'T EXPECT EVERYONE TO FOLLOW MY REQUEST, BUT I ALSO hadn't expected that only half of the pack would. The half who stayed in their homes and refused to move were older wolves who didn't want to leave the only place they knew.

I honestly didn't have the patience to deal with them. So I let it slide, at least for a couple more hours. That time was more for myself, so I would calm down and not drag them out by their arms, than to have them change their minds.

After the Whitecrest challenge and my request, my friends acted. First, they packed their stuff while everyone else did too, then they grabbed any cars they could find and started filling them with everyone and everything. Dom and Vallin went from house to house, asking wolves if they were ready and helping them either fill up their own cars, or hop in theirs.

Evelyn and Ash did the same, though she was explicit that as soon as they had helped us evacuate, they would come back. They wanted to free the dragon, even if the poison had gotten to him. I told her she could do whatever she wanted, as long as everyone was safely away from here.

Killian and Lavinia were in charge of taking all the important paperwork from the town hall and the library—documents, records, archives, anything that we could use later to help us rebuild. Almae did the same with whatever we had for potions and magical spells, things that might come in handy when we were homeless.

Meanwhile, Raika and I helped Jay pack all the essentials from the infirmary and prepare the sick people. Dom and I brought over the two biggest SUVs we could find in town, and loaded them up—Minsi and Lucille included. Some of them were awake and conscious while we transported them from the infirmary's beds to the car seats. They asked what was going on, where we were taking them, and said they didn't want to leave.

I reassured them it was for the best.

I just hoped I wasn't lying to them.

Roman drove one SUV; Jay drove the other. Rue and Vianna followed in separate cars, taking all the kids with them.

Raika and I stood in the middle of Main Street, watching as they left. Raika put a hand over her heart and inhaled deeply. I knew what she felt because I felt the same. I hated seeing them leaving, but what other choice did I have? I couldn't protect them here.

"She'll be fine," I said.

Raika nodded. "I know, but it's still not easy."

It pained me to see Minsi leaving with them. But Rue and Tyren—

My thoughts came to a halt.

I glanced around. I had told Tyren to go with them, but I

couldn't remember seeing him in any of the cars. "Where's Tyren?"

"He was ..." Raika frowned. "I swear I saw him here a few minutes ago. But—"

"He tricked us. He was here so we would see him, but he didn't go with them."

Raika's eyes widened. "Where is he, then?"

We looked around again, but it looked like a ghost town from here. The streets were empty, and there were fewer lights on than usual. The wolves who remained were inside their homes, probably sleeping by now as if nothing had happened.

I could only think that Tyren was at our house, playing video games, acting like the other wolves who were giving me a headache.

I picked up my phone and tried calling him, but he didn't answer. "Why is he being a pain in my ass right now?"

"Hey, it's okay." Raika turned to me, one of her hands on my arm. "We'll find him. We can separate and search for him."

I wanted to argue that Raika should leave too. I should too. I had agreed to meet Nortrix south of here. I could go with everyone else, sleep a few hours at the inn, try to recharge, and then meet him for the challenge.

But I had to admit, I also didn't want to leave. Not yet. Not while I still could hold on to this place and what it meant to me.

Raika went to my house, while I searched the infirmary, the town hall, and the library. If any of us found Tyren, we would text each other. The moment I found him, he would get an earful. If he so much as argued with me, I would give him an alpha command. There was no time to joke around.

I entered my office in the town hall and paused. A lot of the paperwork was gone, but there were still a few things I could take with me: my family portrait on the counter behind the desk. The fountain pen my mother had given my father on his fortieth birthday. A card Minsi had made him for Father's Day, that he had kept in one of the drawers, even though we didn't celebrate most special dates like humans did. And a couple of other things that had sentimental value. It felt silly and at the same time necessary to take those with me.

I heard footsteps outside my office and stiffened. "Tyren?" I asked out loud, though from the heavy boots sound clanking on the hard floor, I knew it wasn't.

Delco appeared at the door.

My muscles tensed at once. "What are you doing here?" Whatever it was, it couldn't be good.

Delco strolled in. "I heard what happened." I frowned. Already? "Nortrix issued you a challenge. That's quite the bold move."

I crossed my arms. "He's trying to take me down while I'm weak. Or at least, while he thinks I am weak."

One of Delco's eyebrows cocked up. "Well, from where I'm standing, he's right."

I didn't like where this conversation was going. "My pack has had some misfortune, but you shouldn't worry about it. I have it under control." What a shitty lie.

"If you say so." His eyes settled on the portrait in my hands. "Your father was a strong alpha. Ruthless. He didn't hesitate to do what was right."

A growl started in my chest. "Delco, I doubt you've come here to gloat. So tell me, what the hell are you doing here?"

He lifted his chin. "I came to collect what you owe me."

Shit. "The favor. Delco, I don't know if you noticed, but I'm in no condition to leave my pack and help you with whatever you want."

"Oh, but what I want is nothing you can't do."

"What is it?"

"Nortrix's challenge. I want you to lose it."

It took me a second to make sense of his words. "You want me to lose to Nortrix? You're asking me to let him kill me?"

"Yes, I am."

Anger became a heavy ball in my torso. "Why?" It wasn't as if Delco would benefit if Nortrix won. What would he gain if Nortrix became the alpha over my broken pack and cursed pack lands?

"That ... is none of your business." He strolled to the door, but paused under the doorjamb. "I think my request is simple."

"And what if I don't accept?"

The gleam in Delco's eyes darkened. "Then, you'll be at war with me too."

A minute after Delco left, I got a text from Raika saying Tyren was at my house, packing all of his video games and electronics. He was pissed, but who wasn't?

I now had to find another ride for him. Or I could drive him and Raika to the nearest town so they could join the others. I would probably sleep there with them, if I could rest with all the tension rolling over my shoulders, and tomorrow go from there to the meeting place.

And then what? I would fight Nortrix with all I had and try to win, or would I do as Delco asked and lose?

On one hand, if I won, my people would be safe from Nortrix, but the Whitecrest pack would be absorbed into the Nightshade. My people didn't seem too happy with me as it was, and then suddenly I would have a lot of reluctant wolves under my thumb. Not to mention, I would be going against Delco's request, forsaking the deal we had made, and he would declare war against us—a pack on the edge of collapse.

On the other hand, if I let Nortrix win, I would die. My pack would be absorbed into Whitecrest, and only the moon knew how Nortrix and his wolves would treat them. There would be no one here to fight for them, to defend them. Besides, the thought of leaving Raika and my siblings behind at the hands of such a cruel alpha made my chest hurt.

This was an impossible choice, but one that I had to make by the time I faced Nortrix tomorrow morning.

Feeling heavy and confused, I grabbed the few items I had collected, put them in a box to be easier to carry, and walked out of the town hall.

My phone dinged again.

I held the box in one hand and checked my phone.

I started reading the text and halted.

Change of plans. Challenge at midnight. See you then. Nortrix.

I stared at the screen as if the words could suddenly change.

Tonight? I would barely have time to take Raika and Tyren to the inn, and check on Minsi and the other sick wolves, before I had to leave for the challenge.

By the moon.

I hurried my steps. On my way down Main Street, I glanced side to side. A handful of houses still had their lights on. Shit. If Dom and Vallin didn't have to come with me to the challenge, I would have requested they come back here. Someone had to talk to these wolves and make them leave before they fell sick. Maybe I could ask Raika to do that. Most wolves had trusted her while I was gone. Did they still trust her?

There was only one way to find out.

When I arrived at my house, I found Raika in the driveway, carrying some boxes to the truck's bed—my father's truck had been totaled when the Whitecrest wolves attacked us a couple of days ago, but Kortan had had one. Since he couldn't use it anymore, we borrowed it.

"Everything okay over here?" I asked as I approached her. I dropped the box I was carrying in the bed too.

Raika narrowed her eyes. "Define okay."

I scoffed. "Fair."

She gestured toward the house. "I feel this urge to pack everything, but I know we don't have time for that." She patted the truck. "But I've got a lot of Minsi's things. Clothes, toys, books. I thought she would need them to make a better transition to wherever it is we're going after all of this."

I nodded, not trusting my voice, my words. It was one thing for me to go into a challenge with the intention to win —though I wasn't so sure about that yet—but another to actually win. Nortrix was older and more experienced than I was.

"We'll figure everything out."

Raika looked at me. Her bright blue eyes filled with tears. "Right. Hm, we should get Tyren and go." She walked away before I could see her crying.

An invisible hand squeezed my heart.

After a few more minutes and a dozen more boxes and

suitcases, Tyren hopped in the backseat, Raika sat in the passenger seat, and I slipped behind the wheel.

Slowly, I drove down the driveaway and stopped the truck once we were on the main street. The three of us stared at the house. This could be the last time we saw it.

I inhaled deeply. "Ready?"

Raika nodded. Tyren stared at me through the rearview mirror, then put on his headphones and closed his eyes.

I put the truck in drive and drove.

26

SHANE

DARK CLOUDS HID THE STARS AND THE THIRD QUARTER MOON from view. In a handful of days, it would be full. Every day now, I could feel the Shadow Wolf growing more agitated, especially when I was angry.

If I won the challenge, we would have to find a safe place where I could be locked up, because I was sure the Shadow Wolf would show up at least one night sooner, and probably last one night longer.

It was happening as the Nightmist witches said it would. The Shadow Wolf was becoming stronger.

There was one easy way for me to win the challenge: to let my Shadow Wolf take over. But would that be fair? Would that count? It had counted with Conri because he had been a bastard and I had been the rightful heir.

I hadn't made up my mind yet.

The thirty-minute drive was quiet and tense. We arrived at the roadside inn and it was unsettling to see so many cars in the parking lot. We parked the truck, climbed out, and Dom came to meet us.

"Most wolves are already in their rooms," he reported. "I've got two adjacent rooms for the sick wolves. Jay said he'll get a mattress and sleep with them." He offered me a key. "This is yours." Then he turned to Tyren. "And you're with me. Come on."

"Wait," I said. I glanced at the number on the key, then handed the key to Raika. "Why don't you take Tyren up? I have some things to talk to Dom about."

Raika frowned but nodded. She probably knew I wasn't hiding anything from her. I was doing this for Tyren.

Dom grabbed his key and offered it to Tyren, but Tyren crossed his arms and didn't take it. It hadn't been three weeks since we had been reunited, but he had shown me his moody teenage side only a couple of times. This was one of them.

"Tyren," I started.

"What?" he barked. "I'm supposed to just go to the room and sleep as if nothing was happening? I know you. You'll leave for your challenge in the middle of the night and you won't even say goodbye to me. And who knows, maybe it really is goodbye this time? What if—?"

I pulled him to me and embraced him tight. "I get that you're mad at me, at everything that is happening, but you have to try keeping a good head about your shoulders." He pushed against me, but I held on tight. "It's true, I might not come back from the challenge, and if I don't, I'll need you to be strong. For Minsi, for Raika, for everyone." A ball got stuck in my throat. "And remember that no matter what, I love you."

Tyren's body slackened against mine and he finally embraced me too. A sob rose from his chest, but he silenced it. "Just ... come back. Okay? Come back."

"I will," I told him, finally knowing what I would do. To

hell with Delco. I would fight Nortrix and I would do anything in my power to win. I couldn't guarantee the outcome, though. I glanced at Raika, and she averted her gaze and wiped at her eyes. "Now go with Raika. I'll see you tomorrow, okay?"

Nodding, Tyren stepped back. He held my gaze for a long beat, then turned and let Raika guide him away.

Dom stepped closer to me, but he remained quiet, knowing that if we talked now, chances were Raika and Tyren would hear. Once they entered one of the rooms, Dom looked at me, his brow furrowed. "What is it?"

"The challenge is at midnight."

"What?" He picked up his phone and checked the time. "But that's ... too soon."

Didn't I know it? "Where's Vallin?"

"Patrolling the area around the inn, making sure no Whitecrest wolf or other threats are around."

I nodded. "You and Vallin have to come with me to the challenge, as witnesses. I'll ask Killian to have some of his vampires keep an eye on the inn while we are gone." I was going to text Killian and ask him and Lavinia to accompany Raika back into Nightshade. I didn't want her in town alone. "I need to talk to Raika, so meet me down here in an hour."

"What if Tyren sees me leaving?"

"Tell him it's your turn to patrol."

Dom nodded.

We headed into the inn together. Dom showed me to the room where Jay was with Minsi and the other wolves, then he left for his room.

I knocked on the door.

"Who is it?" Jay asked, his voice low. Careful.

"It's me," I said.

The door flew open and Jay gestured for me to come in. I walked into the bedroom and took it in—a large rectangle with two queen beds and a sleeper sofa, and a door opened to the adjacent room, the exact same layout as this one, only mirrored. Each sick wolf took one of the beds or a sleeper sofa, and Minsi was alone in a queen bed too large for her. Lucille was on the bed to her right.

I sat at the edge of Minsi's bed and touched her frail, darkened hand. Was it too soon to wish she was already recovering? That they all were?

"How are they?"

Jay sighed. "Th-the same. Though two of them seemed to wake up about an hour ago. They asked for water, said their fingers burned, their head hurt, and then fell back asleep."

"Keep giving them Lavinia's potion. And if Lavinia comes up with something else to give them, trust her."

"Y-yes." Jay frowned. "But you're coming back, right?"

I stared at my sister for another moment. Then I pushed to my feet and placed a hand on Jay's shoulder. "I'll do my best." He nodded and shrank into himself. "Take care of them," I told him. "And be safe."

I walked out of the bedroom and headed for my own. I was about to text Killian and let him know my plan when he stepped in front of me and I almost bumped into him.

"Damn, vampire," I muttered. My nerves were piling up. Here was one more see-you-soon that might have a more finite ending to it. "I was about to text you."

He frowned. "What happened?"

I told him about the time change and what I wanted him to do. His expression grew dark as I spoke. "Hopefully, I'll be back before you."

"I don't like this," he said. "Why did he change the time?"

"Does it matter?"

"I also don't like that I can't come with you."

"Rules are rules. Only wolves, preferably betas, as witnesses. Besides, I would rather you stay with Raika. The worst that could happen is people not answering their doors, since it's late, or shutting the door in her face, but still ... I'll feel better knowing you're with her."

Killian nodded. He grasped my forearm. "Be careful, and kill the damn bastard."

I chuckled, though there was no humor in it. "Take care, my friend."

Killian nodded again. He zipped out of view. I was really tired of goodbyes and there was one more, the most painful of all, for me to go through.

I halted in front of my bedroom door. I knocked, and three seconds later, Raika opened the door.

"Hey." She stepped back and let me in. "I just got back from Tyren's room. He's going to be moody for days."

I walked in and closed the door behind me.

Raika grabbed one of the bags from the desk and opened it. "I brought one of Minsi's bags to the room. I thought I could help her change into something clean once she feels better."

"Raika."

"Because she'll feel better soon, right? We're out of the pack lands now, away from the crystals and the poison. She and the others will be good in no time."

"Raika."

She picked up a pink shirt from the bag. "I think she'll like this one. You know what we could do once she's better? Take her shopping. In a human town. I think she'll love that."

I stepped right into her space and held her hands in mine.

"Raika," I whispered. She pressed her lips together, her eyes scanning everything in the room but me. "Hey." I put a finger under her chin and lifted. Finally her eyes met mine, the blue in them radiating because of the unshed tears. "The challenge is at midnight."

"W-what?" She stepped back. "No, that's too soon."

I held her hands tighter and pulled her back to me. "Listen to me. I promise you, I'll do my best to win. For you, for Tyren, for Minsi, and for the rest of the pack. I don't want to lose any of you again and I won't let you lose me either. We're a family and we'll be together. I know things are a mess right now, but together, we'll figure out a way to make everything right again."

A tear rolled down her cheek. "I don't want you to go."

"You know I have to. I can't deny a challenge."

"I know," she whispered.

"Since I know you won't be able to sleep, I have a job for you. While I'm gone, please go back into town and convince the ones who stayed behind to leave with you."

She scoffed. "After the fiasco in the square, I doubt they will listen to me."

"Remind them that not long ago, they depended on you for everything, and you took great care of them with limited resources. And now, if they let you, you'll take care of them again."

She pouted. "Did you rehearse that?"

"Not really, but I might add it to my list of future speeches," I joked and she snorted. "That will keep your body and your mind occupied while I'm gone."

Another tear escaped her eyes. I brought my hand up, cupped her face, and wiped the tear away with my thumb.

She held on to my wrist. "How long do you have?"

"Long enough for you," I whispered a second before pressing my mouth to hers.

Her lips parted and I kissed her. Her mouth molded to mine as I took the kiss slow and deep, savoring her sweet taste and her intoxicating scent. Desire pooled in my pants and it was suddenly uncomfortable inside my jeans.

By the moon, I needed her.

I ran my hands down her body and reached for her shorts. I would love to take everything slow, but unfortunately, I didn't have the time for that. I yanked the button and zipper open and pushed her shorts down. Next, I tugged at her tank top. We broke the kiss long enough for me to pull the top over her head and throw it aside. Taking advantage of the brief pause, I pulled my shirt off too. Then her mouth was on mine again, her breasts pressed against my chest, her skin warm against mine. I splayed my hands on her back, holding her tight against me for a moment, then I reached for her bra's clasp.

Raika pulled back before I could undo it. She stared at me with those brilliant blue eyes, her lips tilted up. "I have something for you."

She deftly unzipped my jeans and pulled them down, just enough to free my aching hard-on. Then she knelt in front of me.

Holy shit ...

Raika closed her hand around my shaft and I sucked in a sharp breath. She pressed a soft kiss to the tip of my length and I groaned. Her warm tongue licked the head of my hard-on and my knees buckled. By the moon ... I reached for the dresser behind me and braced myself. She did that once, twice, three times, a smile on her lips each time my body shook. Then she closed her eyes and took my length into her mouth. All of it.

I stilled, the sensation perfect. As if that wasn't enough, Raika sucked and moved her hand along with her mouth. Her lips made a loud pop when she released me, and I had never heard a more satisfying noise. She took my length into her mouth again and started moving, taking me in and out of her mouth, her hand following along. It started steady and delicious, but then she sped up, and I felt the desire building up. If she continued that for too long, we wouldn't have time for the rest.

And I wanted the rest.

I reached for her to make her stop, but then somehow she took me deeper into her mouth, she moved faster, squeezed, and sucked harder. My stomach coiled, my knees buckled, and I knotted my hands in her hair.

Dear moon, this was incredible.

But I wanted more from her than this.

I reached for her hands and pulled back. Raika stopped and looked up at me, confused. "Did I do something wrong?"

Chuckling, I helped her stand. "By the moon, no. Nothing wrong. In fact, it was fucking perfect." I pushed my pants all the way down and stepped out of them, then I finally got rid of Raika's bra and panties. I wound my arm around her waist and pulled her to me. "But if I'm not mistaken, I promised you something not long ago."

I steered us back, until her back hit the wall. Her mouth formed an O and shit, that alone was a turn on.

Holding her gaze, I cupped Raika's round ass, pulled her up a little, and entered her. I groaned as delicious friction pressed around my length. She was so damn tight and wet; I pushed in until I couldn't go anymore and stopped, the sensation rolling down my spine. By the moon, it was so damn good to be inside her. Raika held my shoulders and knotted her legs around my waist, angling her hips toward mine, taking me even deeper. She moaned, her lips parted. I groaned and I bit down on her lower lip.

"You're so fucking perfect," I said before claiming her mouth and kissing her. She wiggled her hips and I took the hint. I smiled against her lips as I started moving. Slowly at first, trying to enjoy every second of this, committing it to memory, holding it forever in my mind and heart ... just in case I didn't come back tomorrow.

But it was too good. I wanted more. I needed more. I sped up, thrusting into her deeper and harder. Her body tensed with every thrust, the desire building up. I held on to her, spun us around, and lowered her to the queen bed, my body still glued to her. I started moving again as soon as we were on the mattress, but Raika pushed my shoulders back. I slowed down and looked at her.

"I love you," she said, her voice thick with emotion.

My heart squeezed. "I—"

She lifted her entire body up and whirled us in bed. She pushed me down on the mattress and straddled me, her long, wavy hair like a thick curtain around her shoulders. With a wicked smile, she rested her hands on my chest and started moving.

I groaned as the friction changed, but was just as delicious. For someone who had been a virgin until not long ago, Raika sure did know how to please a guy. I was damn happy I was that guy.

She straightened her spine, her hands on my stomach, as she moved up and down, taking me deep inside her. The tension was back, along with the pressure building up.

I reached up, cupped her plump breasts, and rubbed my thumbs over her nipples. Raika hissed and sped up some more. I jerked as I felt it. I was so damn close.

I closed my hands around her waist, pulling her down toward me, and I moved my hips in rhythm with hers, helping her take me deeper—not that she needed it. Her walls clenched around my length and she gasped. I sped up a little more and she followed for five seconds. She moaned and her body broke in little trembles. She fell over me and her lips met mine. The kiss, her breasts on my chest, her warm core around my length—it took me over the edge. I locked my arms around her and groaned as I came, stronger than ever before.

I shook for a few more seconds, then I pulled back enough to look into her eyes. "I love you too."

She smiled at me.

I reached up and kissed her again. I didn't mean to, but I was sure my apprehension was clear through the kiss. I dragged my lips across her jaw, down her throat, and buried my head on her neck. I inhaled deeply, taking in as much of her sweet scent as I could, and kept my arms around her.

If it depended on me, I would never let her go.

AFTER MAKING LOVE TO RAIKA, I didn't dwell. I got up, got dressed, said a quick goodbye and left. Because I had no strength left to do it any other way.

If I took my time, if I held her, if I told her I loved her again, I wasn't sure I would be able to leave.

I walked out of the room and closed the door behind me. I paused for a second and took a deep breath. I heard her sniffle from inside the room and marched away before the sound broke my resolve.

I was five minutes early, but so were Dom and Vallin. They waited for me by Vallin's truck. When they saw me approaching, they didn't say anything. Vallin slipped behind the wheel, Dom took the backseat, and I climbed into the passenger seat.

And off we went.

The inn was an hour south of the pack lands, and the meeting place was one hour south from the inn. With Vallin's heavy foot, we were able to shave off a few minutes.

At eleven fifty, we arrived at the meeting place. This time, there was no tent, and so far, no one else around. Vallin left the headlights on, pointing to the clearing, so we could see something.

My skin tingled and my stomach knotted. I didn't want to admit it, but I was nervous. To pass the time and to try to relax, I stretched. Dom and Vallin walked the clearing's perimeter, searching for danger.

Midnight came.

And no one showed up.

Had I understood him wrong? I glanced at my phone. Nope, the text said midnight. I texted him.

Where are you?

I paced while I waited for an answer.

A minute passed.

Then two.

Nortrix, are you fucking with me?

No answer.

Dom walked to my side. "Are you talking to him? What's going on?"

"He's not answering."

Just then, my phone dinged.

I'll be there soon.

Dom read the text over my shoulder. "He's late? Really?"

Vallin stood a few feet away, his back to us, his eyes on the clearing. "This doesn't smell good."

I had that same sense. "To the hell with this." I called Nortrix. The phone rang and rang. "Something is wrong." I tried calling him again. On the third ring, he answered it.

"You're still there?" he asked, sounding bored.

"Yes."

"Good. Then, have fun." He turned off the call.

I stared at my phone. "What the hell was that?"

Howls filled the air.

A second later, wolves with white spots appeared in the clearing, illuminated by the truck's headlights. Fifteen of them.

"Oh, shit," Dom muttered.

He and Vallin stepped closer to each other. We turned back-to-back and faced the wolves as they closed a circle around us.

The wolves lunged at us and we barely had time to shift. Mad about the deception, my Shadow Wolf asked for release, but I was afraid that without Raika here to tame him, I could end up hurting Dom or Vallin.

I called on my black wolf before the shadow one could take control.

Hold your position, I told Dom and Vallin through our mental link.

Three wolves rushed us, followed closely by three more—two for each of us. I sidestepped the first wolf and met the second one head on. I swiped at his muzzle, hitting him hard and sending him sideways, over the first one. The two of them became a heap at my paws and I took advantage of the moment. I closed my teeth around the first wolf's neck.

The second wolf yelped and jumped to his feet. But I was ready for him. I bit down on his ear and ripped it off. He yelped again as I spit it out. I smacked at his back and pinned him down. I ripped his throat open.

When I looked up, I found Dom and Vallin had disposed of the other four.

All right. Six down, nine to go, I said into Dom and Vallin's minds.

Three other wolves came at me. I jumped out of the way before they got too close. I turned to them and snarled. This was taking too long. Whatever game Nortrix was playing, I wanted out of it.

I felt my Shadow Wolf within an arm's reach. I had tapped into him before, when Serge was harassing Raika, and hadn't lost control. Granted, Raika had been there.

But I had to trust my gut, and my gut told me I needed to finish this fast.

I welcomed a fraction of the Shadow Wolf. Shadows swirled around me and I suddenly stood on two legs, not four.

The three wolves hesitated.

I didn't. I ran to them. One jumped at me as I got close, but I simply extended my hand, grabbed him by the neck, and flung him to a tree. The wolf hit the tree and fell with a sickening crunch.

The second one ran at me, but I held it by the neck and rump and broke his spine. The wolf howled. I dropped him on the ground beside me like flicking lint off my clothes.

The third wolf yelped and ran away from me.

Right. I ran after him, and in five steps, I reached him. I

smacked my hand on his side and he rolled away. Before he could get up, I stepped on his ribs, cracking a few, and struck his neck with my claws. Deep gashes cut his throat and blood oozed out.

For a second, I rejoiced in the destruction. I wanted more.

I shook my head and stepped back. No, this wasn't me. I was done with this wolf for now. If I stayed in this half-form longer, no one would be safe.

I inhaled deeply and thought of Raika, of how even my Shadow Wolf liked her. She could calm me down, bring me joy, make everything all right.

Slowly, the remains of the Shadow Wolf left me and I was my plain black wolf again.

I turned back to the fight, expecting to be attacked right away.

But there were only two wolves left and Dom and Vallin had them.

Vallin yelped and fell, blood staining from his back.

Vallin, what happened? I asked, rushing to him.

Vallin groaned as the wolf pinned him down.

I halted in shock as the wolf bit down on Vallin's neck. Enraged, I snapped out of my shock and charged at him, pushing him away from my beta. I clamped down on his muzzle with my paw, then closed my teeth around his head, sinking my teeth deep. The wolf yelped and then went limp.

I turned to Vallin. His wolf shuddered and he shifted back to his human form. I shifted too and knelt beside him. My stomach knotted at the blood oozing from his wound. I pressed a hand on it, but it was futile.

"I-I'm sorry," he uttered.

"Hey, hey. You're okay. You'll be fine," I lied. "There's nothing to be sorry about. You're a good beta." Vallin gasped, but his throat was probably filling up with blood. He shook once more, then stopped. His arms fell heavy to his sides and his eyes stared at nothing. I closed his eyes. "Rest in peace."

"Here!" Dom yelled. He had one of the Whitecrest wolves, the last one, pinned to the ground.

I rushed to them. The Whitecrest wolf had a deep wound on his stomach and had shifted to his human form because of that. He trembled from head to toe, just like Vallin had a minute ago. I didn't have long to make him talk.

I leaned over him. "Answer me and I'll stop your suffering. Don't answer and I'll make you suffer more, but I won't let you die."

The wolf gasped. "You fell for it," he said, a tone between breathless and amused.

"I fell for what?"

"The challenge. Coming here. Nortrix knew we might not kill you, but at least we got you away from Nightshade."

A cold chill coursed through my veins. "My pack?"

"No, the town."

"Why?"

The wolf laughed, his teeth stained with blood. His laughter turned into a cough, then a gag. "You're too late now," he muttered, spitting blood with each word. His eyes rolled back and his body stilled.

Dread punched me in the chest, robbing me of air. I stared at Dom. "We've got to go. Now!"

We picked up Vallin's body and put him in the truck's bed. Then we climbed in and peeled away from the clearing, wheels singing.

27

RAIKA

I let myself cry for a full minute after Shane left.

Then I sprang into action.

Shane was right. If I stayed in the inn's room by myself, wondering about his damn challenge, I would go crazy within minutes.

I got dressed, washed my face, brushed my hair, and walked to the parking lot. To my surprise, Killian, Lavinia, Almae, Evelyn, Ash, and Roman were already there, beside a large SUV.

"What are you all doing here?" I asked.

"Shane told me to take you to town," Killian said. "When the others learned about it, they volunteered to go with us."

"But ..."

"No buts," Roman said. He opened the SUV's back door. "Come on. The sooner we go, the sooner we come back."

I nodded and hopped in the third row. He sat in the back with me.

In less than a minute, we were all inside the SUV and driving toward our pack lands. The hour-long drive was tough. My friends tried making small talk, but what could we talk about when everything had changed so much in such a short time?

I couldn't even wrap my head around it all. Dixon had played with us and handed us poisoned crystals, which were now killing our land and making our people sick. But Dixon had been a pawn. Someone else was behind it, giving the orders, laughing as we suffered. But who?

Then there was the dragon, the Whitecrest's challenge, Shane's uncured curse, and my demon father.

Oh, and now everyone knew I was mated to Shane. Not only that, but they knew I was half-demon. I wasn't one bit ashamed of being Shane's mate, but I was mortally embarrassed about being a half-demon. The wolves who were already glancing at us sideways, because of all the mounting problems and no visible solutions, now plain distrusted us.

By the moon, couldn't things be a little simpler?

As Killian stopped the SUV in the middle of Main Street, where a few houses still had their lights on. We all got out of the SUV and huddled together.

"What is the plan?" Evelyn asked.

"I think Raika and Roman should do the talking," Lavinia said. "We're just here to watch out if any trouble arises."

Killian nodded. "The wolves are used to you two. If we, the outsiders, try to step in, that might close them off more."

I glanced at Roman and he nodded at me.

"Here goes nothing," I muttered.

Roman went south, I went north. The rest divided in half and followed us from a safe distance.

As I turned toward the first house, I glanced up to the sky. Clouds covered the sky again, and it was dark out, even for the middle of the night.

I knocked on the door. I heard shuffling inside, but no one opened the door. I knocked again. "It's Raika. I'm here to talk. Please open the door."

Moon, I hoped they answered, because if they didn't, then … what? I had to leave them here until they too fell sick from the poison? That wasn't an option.

An old lady opened the door. Lydia was her name. She had lost her mate, her sister, and one of her sons during the first attack. She lost her other son and her nephew during the second attack.

My heart hurt for her.

"I'm not going anywhere," she said, her tone resolute. "My family died here. I'll die here too."

"I understand but—" A loud scraping sound caught my attention. Several feet behind me, Killian and Lavinia stiffened. "What was that?" I asked.

"I'll go see," Killian said. "Stay here."

He zoomed out of sight. Apprehension laced around my chest. "Lydia, go back inside. Close the door. And please, pack. I'll be back to take you with me soon." I pointed my finger at her. "No argument."

She opened her mouth, but I didn't stay to hear her. I walked to Lavinia, who stood very still in the middle of the street, looking at the darkness stretching beyond us. A few lights flickered farther ahead, where the main square was located.

I narrowed my eyes. "Can you see anything?" My regular vision was better than a human's, but it was nothing compared to when I was in wolf form. But for Lavinia, all she had to do was focus.

She shook her head. "Just some shadows, but I think that's the lights playing tricks."

Another scraping sound came from the square. My stomach knotted. "Where's Killian? We should go after him."

Lavinia nodded.

Slowly, the two of us made our way toward square. With each step, our sight adjusted to the dark and slowly, the square took shape. Lavinia and I walked closer. We halted a few feet from the square's edge and looked around.

There was nothing here.

Nothing to make the scraping noise. And no Killian.

The streetlamps around the square flickered and came to life.

I gasped and grasped Lavinia's wrist.

Wolves with white spots stalked from the darkness toward us. At least two dozen of them, if not more. Three of them, in human form, held Killian by his arms. Killian had his head low, his lips split.

Lavinia thrummed under my hold. Black lines appeared around her eyes and she bared her fangs. "Let him go!"

"I'm not so sure I can do that," a voice said.

Nortrix, in human form and fully clothed, appeared from behind his wolves. When he stepped into the square, more wolves appeared behind us, caging us in.

Shit.

"Wait. The challenge? You're not supposed to be here."

Nortrix smirked. "I'm right where I need to be."

My stomach sank. "What does that mean? What did you do to Shane?"

"If it all goes according to plan, he's beaten and tied up, being watched by my wolves, and waiting until I'm done so I can kill him and claim his pack."

I shook my head. "I don't understand."

He grinned, a creepy thing that chilled my bones. "You

will. But for now, all I can do is thank you. You've made my life easier. I thought that once I was done here, I would have to go after you, but look at that!" He gestured toward me. "Here you are!"

Nothing about this made sense. "What are you talking about?"

"He's trying to bait you," Lavinia whispered. "Don't fall for it."

"Easier said than done," I whispered back. But it was damn hard. "What do we do? We can't take them all by ourselves."

"I say we buy time until our friends realize what's happening, then we get out of here. There's no way we can fight them all and win."

"What are you two whispering about?" Nortrix asked, that creepy smile still on his face. "You aren't planning on leaving, are you? Don't even try. Soon, there will be no way out of here."

I frowned and almost asked him again what the hell he was doing, but saved my voice. It wasn't like he would answer anyway.

"Raika!"

"Lavinia!"

The two of us turned toward the voices and saw our friends—Roman, Almae, Evelyn, and Ash—running toward us. They slowed down and stopped when several of the Whitecrest wolves snarled.

Nortrix tsked. "No funny business. Everyone stay where you are. This will be over soon." He walked away from us, toward the gap in the square's center.

Hushes reached my ears. Behind my friends, I could see people peeking from inside their houses. I wanted to tell them to go back inside, but I was afraid that if I did that, Nortrix would use them against me.

"What are those?" Lavinia asked.

I snapped my attention back to Nortrix. He walked in a wide arc beside the gap, placing what looked like black crystals on the ground.

Nortrix didn't answer her. He placed a fifth crystal on the ground and stepped back.

Shiny black lines appeared on the ground, from crystal to crystal, like they had been carved out by laser. They connected to each other, touching all of the crystals and forming a web of dark light. A spot above the center of the crystal imploded and a small black ball appeared in the middle of the air. It expanded until it was bigger than a door.

Lavinia gasped. "A portal."

"Precisely," Nortrix said, his eyes on the shiny black portal.

A moment later, someone stepped through it.

A tall man with olive skin, dark brown curls, and bright blue eyes. He wore a neat black suit and fancy shoes, and he seemed like a fish out of water. He turned to Nortrix.

Nortrix bowed his head to the man. "My prince. Everything is going according to your plan."

I gasped. So Nortrix, alpha of the Whitecrest pack, was working for someone else? Someone powerful and intimidating.

Then a memory sparked to life in my mind: Almae had told us a great evil would come. I thought it was the dragon, but now I wasn't so sure.

"Good," the man said, his voice deep. He glanced around, and narrowed his eyes at my friends and me. "What are those?"

What, not who. The bastard.

"Nuisances, my prince," Nortrix said. "After you're done here, I'll dispose of them. But not all." He pointed a long finger at me. "We agreed I would retrieve her after your stop here, but she showed up by herself, saving me the trip."

He waved at Nortrix, who bowed again and disappeared to the square's edge. The man turned to me, his eyes on mine. "Excellent."

I took a step back as my hackles raised. This man exuded power and malice, and all I wanted was distance from him.

Lavinia grabbed my arm and pulled me half behind her. I appreciated the gesture, but I wouldn't cower, even if I had to muster courage from thin air.

"W-what do you want with me?" I forced my throat to work.

The man pressed a hand to his chest. "Let me introduce myself. I'm Prince Paimon of the underworld."

Lavinia snorted. "You're not a prince anymore. You were demoted and ran away when Brikan was killed. Now you're just a demon."

He flicked his hand at her. A fast black bolt—darkfire— shot out and hit her chest. Lavinia's eyes widened.

I turned to her, shocked, and examined her, but there was nothing wrong with her, not visibly. "What did you do to her?"

Lavinia opened and closed her mouth, but no words came out.

Paimon clicked his tongue. "That's much better."

Killian yanked against the ones holding him, and our friends yelled and tried advancing, but the wolves pushed them back. I was sure they could come to us if they really wanted, but that would start a bigger fight I wasn't sure we could win.

Paimon looked at me. "Where was I? Oh. Introductions. Why don't we continue?" He gestured toward the space around him. "This is the Nightshade pack, famous for its protective barrier, which is finally gone. If Conri had worked faster, I wouldn't have had to wait a year."

I gaped at him. "Conri ... he was working for you? So, Dixon too? You're the one who sent the poisoned crystals back to us?"

His wicked smile stretched. "Wasn't that fun? I didn't see it firsthand, of course, but the reports told me you tried everything, even awakening the dragon!"

What ... "You know about the dragon?"

"Of course I do. I'm old, my dear. Ancient. I know things that shouldn't be remembered by anyone." He glanced at the gap behind him as if bugs were crawling from the hole, and he couldn't wait to squash them with his feet. Behind the gap, I could see Nortrix still moving around. What was he doing? "Anyway. I even anticipated you lot would try to take the fake crystals out with some big surge of magic, which melted the crystals right away, didn't it?" He glanced around. "But it seems the poison hasn't reached the town's center. Not yet, at least."

I clenched my fists. "Why are you doing this?"

"We're still doing introductions, my dear, but if you're so inclined to know." He turned to Nortrix, just as the alpha walked back to him, carrying two crystals.

"No," I whispered. My stomach dropped. Those were the remaining crystals, the good ones, that had been left intact even with the poison spreading. I frowned. "Wait. How did you open the trap doors?"

Paimon extended his hand.

Nortrix handed him the crystals then faced me. "During the alpha meeting your mate called. I was about to create an excuse to see him at the time, but he came to me. All I had to do was make him mad enough to confront me." He lifted his hand and stared at his fingers. "Then I cut him and stole a few drops of his blood."

"Clever, hm?" Paimon held the crystals, one on each hand. "But you asked why I'm here. For this." He closed his eyes and inhaled. The crystals shone bright, a white light that had me squinting. The light snaked out of the crystals and coiled around Paimon's arms, his shoulders. The crystals dulled until they turned gray. The light snake faded around Paimon's chest. He opened his eyes, and they glowed like the crystals had a second ago. He blinked and they went back to normal. "So much power."

Lavinia grabbed my arm and made me look at her. She moved her mouth, telling me something, but I was terrible at lip reading. I only got the part she mouthed, "He's weak."

"Not anymore," Paimon said. "I might not have my full power back, but the crystals helped. After all, they were four in total."

My brow furrowed. "So you sent Conri here to find the crystals, so you could get some of your power back."

"Exactly." Paimon smiled. "You're a smart girl. Just like your mother was."

I stilled. "You knew my mother?"

"Oh, yes. I sent Conri here to retrieve the crystals for me, but that wasn't all I ordered him to do. I told him to protect you." His wicked smile was back. "I'm not finished with the introductions. Here's the last one: You're Raika, half-wolf, half-demon, and my dear daughter."

My throat went dry, the blood left my face.

No, no. I hadn't heard him right. I shook my head and took a large step back. A wolf pushed his nose against my leg, forcing me to stay in place.

A wave of magic rushed through us and suddenly all hell broke loose. I stood there like a rag doll while my friends advanced on the wolves, and the wolves struck back. Lavinia grabbed my arm and pulled me with her.

Then I woke up from my stupor.

I wouldn't dwell on this insane fact right now; there was no time for that. We had to get out of here.

Lavinia disappeared from my side, using her super speed to rush to Killian, who fought with the three men holding him back. She shot blue bolts at them, making them lose their hold.

Evelyn and Almae fought with magic, and they had the wolves down or limping before even getting to them. Ash had his sword out and hacked at the wolves. Roman shifted and lunged at the wolf coming for him.

I turned and saw Paimon smiling at me, like this was all going according to his plan.

Then the ground shook.

Paimon's eyes widened for a second.

"It's the dragon!" Evelyn shouted. "The crystals are gone and there's nothing holding him back now."

The ground shook harder and the gap widened, swallowing the pavement around it. We all stepped back before it swallowed us too.

The fight seemed to pause as the ground exploded, raining dirt and cement everywhere, and the dragon burst free.

My insides liquefied at the sight before me. A dark green,

almost black, gigantic dragon stood where the main square had been. He turned his big head at us and roared, showing off his hundreds of sharp teeth the size of my forearms, the guttural sound hurting my ears. He opened his wings—I had to duck before the giant thing hit my head—and then he took off toward the dark sky.

I stared at it, completely entrance and stunned.

There really had been a dragon underneath our feet this whole time.

I thought the dragon would fly away, but no, he was enraged and probably wanted revenge. He made a beautiful arc in the sky and flew toward us. His throat turned orange.

Oh, shit.

"Run!" I cried.

The dragon opened his big mouth, blowing fire at us. I felt the heat licking at my back as I ran from the center of the square. The dragon swooped up, but not before leaving a thick path of fire in his wake.

Wolves howled from within the fire. They clambered out, their bodies covered in flames. Horror washed through me as they fell face-first on the ground, their bodies writhing.

Nortrix was one of them.

"He's coming back!" someone yelled.

This time everyone ran.

In his human form, Roman appeared by my side and took my hand in his. "This way."

I went with him, letting him pull me along, since he was faster than me. Still, the heat of the fire touching down warmed my back. I halted at a safe distance, slipped my hand free from Roman's, and glanced over my shoulder and gasped. From here, I couldn't tell exactly, but it looked like the fire now consumed most of the square and a couple of the streets around it. The town hall and the infirmary were also on fire.

My heart sank.

Poison wasn't enough. Now fire was destroying our town. If we had harbored any hopes of someday returning to this place, they were now gone.

The dragon went up again, but now I was sure he would come back and finish us off. Or at least try to.

"We have to leave," I told Roman. I looked for my friends, but couldn't see them from here. The fire had separated us.

I hoped they had the same idea as me; it was time to go.

I turned and ran down one of the side streets, intent on disappearing into the forest. I would take the long way back and come check on my friends.

But as soon as I reached the side street, I halted.

Paimon stood a handful of feet from me, a half smile on his lips. "Where do you think you're going, my child?"

28

SHANE

Dom drove as fast as the truck could go back to the Nightshade pack lands. On the way, I called Raika, I called Killian, but neither of them answered. I hoped it was because of the time. It was past midnight and their phones were probably set to do-not-disturb.

That had to be it.

We crossed the border where once the barrier was, and while we drove by a small hill that broke through the trees, we could see it.

"Is that ..." I gaped.

"The dragon," Dom whispered.

A huge mass of black against the night sky, the dragon dove, opened his mouth, and blew fire over the town.

A lead ball sank into my stomach. "Faster!"

"I'm trying!"

The truck shook as the road zoomed under us. I glanced back at the bed, and felt terrible. Vallin rolled side to side like a sack of potatoes. Once this was over, I would honor him and give him a great ceremony.

"By the moon," Dom whispered once we entered the town proper via Main Street. From here, it looked like a sea of fire had washed over the square and surrounding buildings.

My muscles coiled.

Dom stopped the truck beside the SUV in the middle of the road, and I opened the door and jumped out, shifting midair. I ran in my wolf form toward the fire.

Raika? I called through the mind link. She didn't answer and despair took over. *Anyone else?*

I see Evelyn and Almae up ahead, Dom said in my mind. He was running a few feet behind me.

Evelyn and Almae ducked behind a wall at the edge of the street, firing bolts of magic at Whitecrest wolves who ran from the fire toward them.

"Don't hurt the dragon!" Evelyn cried.

A Whitecrest wolf broke through and jumped at them. Ash appeared from the side, brandishing his sword. He cut down the wolf, and when he saw Dom and me, he pointed the sword to us.

"That's Shane," Evelyn warned.

Ash lowered the sword. "Right."

I yelped, hoping they understood what I wanted to know.

"The fire separated us," Almae said. She pointed west. "Killian and Lavinia went that way." Then she pointed east. "And Roman and Raika went that way."

Dom, get them out of here, I said. *I'll go after the others.*

Dom shifted into his human form. "Let's get out of here."

I didn't wait to see if the others had followed the orders. I ran east. The dragon returned once more, this time blasting his fire past the square and igniting one of the side streets leading north. He was going to destroy the entire town this way.

The heat from the fire brushed against my fur as I took an alley between two buildings and emerged on a side road.

I looked side to side.

There, right at the edge of the fire, was Raika.

And in front of her, a tall man I had never seen before.

I ran to them.

Raika said something and took a step back.

The stranger laughed. He jutted his arm forward, a shadow sword in his hand.

A sword that went through Raika's chest.

No!

I pushed harder, faster, but my rage was uncontrollable. The Shadow Wolf took over. I stood tall and advanced toward the stranger.

Kill, destroy, rip apart.

The stranger saw me coming and ran toward the fire.

Raika gasped and looked down, her eyes wide, as if she couldn't believe it. Shadows rapidly swirled around her, then they were gone.

I skidded to a stop in front of her. Just as fast as it came, the Shadow Wolf left me and I was back in my human form.

Raika's round eyes met mine. Then, they fluttered closed and she fell back.

I wound my arm around her and broke her fall. I knelt on the ground, with Raika's limp body tucked against my chest.

"Raika." My voice broke. I hovered my hand over her chest, over the hole right beside her heart, and the copious amounts of blood seeping out. "No." I pressed two fingers to her neck, but I knew I wouldn't find a heartbeat. Something like a cry tore through my throat. I lowered my head to hers. "Please, don't leave me."

This wasn't real; it couldn't be. Raika was sleeping. She

was hurt. And soon Jay would fix her. Then she would laugh, teasing me about how worried I was. She would look at me with her brilliant, contagious smile, and I wouldn't even be mad at her.

"No," someone said.

I glanced up, my vision blurred because of the tears, but I recognized them. My friends walked toward me.

"Do something!" I shouted. Lavinia knelt beside me, her hand on my shoulder. "Can't you heal her?"

Lavinia shook her head. "I can't bring her back. No one can. I'm sorry."

I had been tortured before, for months, but I would gladly welcome that pain back if it meant the pain I felt now would be gone.

This couldn't be happening.

But as much as I wanted to believe otherwise, the truth was right before me, tucked in my arms, heavy and limp and growing cold.

Raika, my beloved mate, was dead.

29

SHANE

Not long ago, I had stood in the town's square, facing a pyre so we could honor the dead.

And now, I was doing it again.

Only this time, it wasn't in my town.

I glanced over my shoulder, at DuMoir Castle in the distance, the sun setting behind it. This place had meant a lot to me, but I hated to be here. Because being back here meant I hadn't had a nightmare two nights ago.

It meant that Raika was really gone.

The pain in my chest only grew as the time passed, despite everyone telling me it would be all right.

It wouldn't be.

Even though we had evacuated the town before the dragon destroyed it all, even though the sick people were now recovering at a steady rate, even though we were together and had a temporary home, nothing would ever be the same.

It would never be all right again.

I looked at my pack forming a wide semicircle around me. All of them quiet, with their heads low, their shoulders slumped. To the side, Lucille and Rue held a crying Minsi, both of them with tears in their eyes.

Inhaling deeply, I picked up the torch from Dom and faced the three pyres in front of me: one for Raika, one for Vallin, and one for Roman.

I stared at Roman's, the only empty pyre. From what I was told, he fell when running with Raika. He had been consumed by the fire, and we weren't able to recover his body. I placed my hand over the pyre and mentally thanked him for all he had done for the pack and for Raika. I might have been jealous of him, but he had always done his best for Raika, no matter what.

I touched the torch to the pyre and it caught fire.

Next, I walked to Vallin. The vampires had cleaned him up and dressed him in an elegant white suit. I had to admit, I didn't know Vallin that well, just that my father had trusted him and had often said that Vallin would have been his choice for a beta, if he ever needed to name another one. In my mind, I thanked him for helping me take care of the pack.

I lowered the torch to the pyre and the flames spread fast.

My throat closed as I walked to Raika. She looked like she was sleeping in her bed of straw, her long black hair spilling around her like a dark halo. Minsi, who had been well but sobbing the whole time, had done a crown of white flowers for her, and the witches had dressed her up in a simple but beautiful white dress. She looked like an angel.

I blinked, fighting the tears. I smoothed my hand down her face, realizing this would be the last time I would ever touch her.

A sob shook my chest.

Tyren stepped closer and pressed a hand to my shoulder.

I looked at him and he was as teary eyed as I was. Once upon a time, I would have cared if people saw me crying.

Now, I wanted to cry and scream.

But first, I had to honor the love of my life. She deserved it.

"I love you," I whispered. "I'll always love you."

I lifted the torch, but I couldn't lower it.

Tyren moved his hand to my arm, as if telling me I wouldn't be doing this alone.

Swallowing another sob, I brought the torch down.

Flames encased the pyre.

I lowered my head and let the tears fall.

SOMEWHERE ELSE
RAIKA

I sat up with a start, breathing hard. I pressed a hand to my chest, a dull pain in my heart. What had happened?

I looked up and found a young woman and a man standing by the bed's footboard, looking at me.

"You're awake!" the man said, his voice deep.

I frowned, my mind spinning and empty.

Where was I? What room was this? Who were these people?

But most importantly... I sucked in a sharp breath. "Who am I?"

Thank you for reading *The Night Burning*! If you liked it, don't forget to pre-order book 3, *The Night Hunting*!

If you haven't yet and would like to read how everything changed for Shane and Raika (aka: Minsi's 10th birthday party, how they found out about the mating bond, and

Conri's attack), then click here to download this exclusive book!

Haven't you read Killian's and Lavinia's story yet? Then download *The Darkest Vampire* and start their trilogy now! That's where Shane is first introduced in the story ;)

Also, join my Facebook group to get another exclusive book, *The Light Witch*. You just met Evelyn and Ash and now you can read their beginning!

Last but not least, you can check out the recommended reading order for the Rite World here! You can download, print, and check the books you've already read! Enjoy!

THANK YOU

Thank you for reading *The Night Burning*!

Reviews are very important for authors. If you liked my book, please consider leaving a review on your favorite online retailer and/or on Goodreads and/or Bookbub, please!

Did you like this book? You can check out other books of mine:

The Darkest Vampire (Rite World: Vampire Wars book 1): a witch releases a dark vampire from a curse, and becomes inadvertently bonded to him.

The Midnight Test (Rite World: Lightgrove Witches book 1): a clueless witch is invited to join a powerful coven—but only if she aces a difficult test.

The Demon Kiss (Rite World: Blackthorn Hunters Academy book 1): a fast-paced story about a young woman who finds out she's a demon hunter, and the half-demon intent on protecting her against all evil.

The Vampire Heir (Rite World 1: Rite of the Vampire): a

dark and mysterious paranormal romance about a vampire and a young woman with a secret.

The Warlock Lord (Rite World 4: Rite of the Warlock): a thrilling and kick-ass paranormal romance about a werewolf and warlock.

The Wolf Forsaken (Rite World 7: Rite of the Wolf): a heat-wrenching tale about a lost wolf shifter and a fae princess on the run.

Heart Seeker (The Fire Heart Chronicles book 1): an urban fantasy series about a young woman who finds herself at the center of a mysterious supernatural world.

Destiny Gift (The Everlast Series book 1): a post-apocalyptic urban fantasy series about a young woman with a special power that can save the world.

DON'T FORGET to sign up for my Newsletter to find out about new releases, cover reveals, giveaways, and more!

If you want to see exclusive teasers, help me decide on covers, read excerpts, talk about books, etc, join my reader group on Facebook: Juliana's Club!

ABOUT THE AUTHOR

While USA Today Bestselling Author Juliana Haygert dreams of being Wonder Woman, Buffy, or a blood elf shadow priest, she settles for the less exciting—but equally gratifying—life as a wife, a mother, and an author. She resides in North Carolina and spends her days writing about kick-ass heroines and the heroes who drive them crazy.

Subscribe to her mailing list to receive emails of announcement, events, and other fun stuff related to her writing and her books: www.bit.ly/JuHNL

For more information:
www.julianahaygert.com

facebook.com/julianahaygert

twitter.com/julianahaygert

instagram.com/juliana.haygert

goodreads.com/juliana_haygert

pinterest.com/julianahaygert

bookbub.com/authors/juliana-haygert

youtube.com/julianahaygert

tiktok.com/@julianahaygert

ALSO BY JULIANA HAYGERT

To find links and more info, go to:

www.julianahaygert.com/books/

Shorts

Into the Darkest Fire

Standalones

Daughter of Darkness

Rite World: Night Wolves

The Night Calling (Book 1)

The Night Burning (Book 2)

The Night Hunting (Book 3)

The Night Rising (Book 4)

Rite World: Vampire Wars

The Darkest Vampire (Book 1)

The Darkest Witch (Book 2)

The Darkest Magic (Book 3)

Rite World: Lightgrove Witches

The Midnight Test (Book 1)

The Midnight Spell (Book 2)

The Midnight Flame (Book 3)

Earth Shaker (Book 2.5)

Sorrow Bringer (Book 3)

Soul Wanderer (Book 4)

Fate Summoner (Book 5)

War Maiden (Book 6)

The Everlast Series

Destiny Gift (Book 1)

Soul Oath (Book 2)

Cup of Life (Book 3)

Everlasting Circle (Book 4)

Willow Harbor Series

Hunter's Revenge (Book 3)

Siren's Song (Book 5)

Breaking Series

Breaking Free (Book 1)

Breaking Away (Book 2)

Breaking Through (Book 3)

Breaking Down (Book 4)